Praise for R

"*Small town life in southern Idaho might seem quaint and idyllic to some. But when local newspaper reporter Cal Murphy begins to uncover a series of strange deaths that are linked to a sticky spider web of deception, the lid on the peaceful town is blown wide open. Told with all the energy and bravado of an old pro, first-timer R.J. Patterson hits one out of the park his first time at bat with* Dead Shot. *It's that good.*"

- *Vincent Zandri, bestselling author of* The Remains

DEAD SHOT

A Novel

R.J. PATTERSON

For Billy Harper, the man who taught me that real newspapermen drink coffee and always print the truth

In the real world, the right thing never happens in the right place and the right time. It is the job of journalists and historians to make it appear that it has.

- Mark Twain

CHAPTER 1

CODY MURRAY SHIFTED IN his recliner as he flipped the pages of his favorite sports magazine. Sitting still wasn't in his repertoire of skills on the field or off it. He lived like he played – always in constant motion.

But it was Sunday afternoon and Cody was trying to relax. He only had two vices, one of which was wasting time reading national sports magazines. The other he had enjoyed 15 minutes earlier. He knew it was wrong, but for an athlete who never stopped, it was the perfect enhancement to his workout regimen. But lately, Cody had become looser with the latter vice, sometimes partaking in it for sheer pleasure.

Cody knew steroids were bad and tough to get, especially in a rural town in southern Idaho. So, he didn't bother trying. He wanted his impressive body of work to be his body of work – he just needed a little help, a little kick while working out. It was harmless ... at first.

Cody dug his jagged fingernails into his left arm in an attempt to remedy a slight itch just above his elbow. It was an irritating distraction from reading the magazine and dreaming of being featured on the cover one day. As unlikely as it might be for the 6-foot-flat scrambling quarterback of a rural Idaho eight-man team to earn a handful of major scholarship offers, Murray had done it. *Why not the cover?* he mused.

But the thoughts abandoned him when the itching started.

At first, it felt like any other itch. Cody expected it to vanish with one quick scratch. But it didn't; it got worse. *What's wrong with me?* he thought, as he surveyed his arms. Red welts were forming on his arms and spreading to his chest and back. All the scratching seemed to make it worse.

In less than a minute his muscular athletic body was covered. All he could think of was getting relief from the fiery pain. Jumping up from the couch, Cody staggered through the back door, taking a giant leap off the deck and then sprinting full speed toward an Aspen tree twenty yards away.

Rational thought had deserted him. He jammed his fingernails into his chest while slamming his back against the tree and began rubbing against it, thrusting upward from a crouching position in an attempt to stop the itching. His efforts only intensified his skin's agitation.

Frantic for relief, Cody raced back into the house, ripping off his Statenville workout shirt along the way, and headed straight for his parents' bathroom. In his mad rush to find anything to help, Cody grabbed a tube of anti-itch cream. He emptied its white contents into his right hand and slathered it all over his bare chest and back. Still no relief. The itching increased.

Cody ran back outside to find another tree. *Maybe with my shirt off, I'll be able to stop the itching.* Past the point of despair, he dug both hands into opposing forearms, fell to the grass and rolled and scratched, crying out in agony.

The intense itching felt like fire searing the surface of his body. Cody screamed and flailed about on the ground in sheer torture. His efforts appeared futile but he refused to give up.

His body was covered in bleeding welts as he writhed in the grass. One final spasmodic convulsion and the itching stopped. So did his breathing. Streaks of blood created eerie patterns across his chest. His body lay in the Idaho sun looking like the discarded carcass of a sadistic occult ritual.

No one would believe that Cody Murray, Statenville's greatest football star in 50 years, had scratched himself to death.

CHAPTER 2

CAL MURPHY'S IPHONE VIBRATED on his bed stand and Cal barely moved. He relished the idea of sleeping in every day, one of the few perks afforded underpaid reporters at a newspaper that only published once a week. But it was a luxury that all but vaporized at 8:30 on this Monday morning in the middle of August.

He fumbled for his phone with the sole purpose of discovering who would absorb his immediate wrath. *Josh Moore... why is that freak calling me so early? He knows I don't do mornings, much less Monday mornings!*

Cal pressed talk and mumbled a hello.

"Good morning, Cal!" came the cheery voice on the other end. "I thought I would call you on the way to work and see if you've got everything planned for my visit next weekend."

Cal moaned.

"Do you have any idea what time it is, Josh?" Cal asked, his morning voice croaked as he tried to shift to a more awake version of himself. "Have you forgotten how much I hate mornings, especially Mondays?"

Josh only smiled, hoping Cal couldn't detect it over the phone.

"Oh, wow, look at the time. I didn't realize it was so early. I would've never called if I thought about it."

"Liar!"

"I'm just messin' with you, Cal. But you need to get motivated to get out of that dump of a town where no real news ever happens so you can get up here to Seattle. You're never going to escape East Bumble when your best clip is an article on the little league tournament champions just below a grip-and-grin photo. Cal – or should I say @CalMurphy24 – you've got seven followers on Twitter. So, get going, OK?"

Cal stared at his vintage poster of Ken Griffey Jr. in a Mariners uniform, a relic from his high school days. He had faithfully tacked it to a wall in every living quarters he had since leaving home. It was even in the dorm room he shared with Josh at the University of Washington their freshman year. When it came to vintage Mariners, Josh preferred Randy Johnson. Quiet, calculated, and never quite living up to others astronomical expectations vs. bold, brash, and making the best use of every ounce of talent he had. Griffey vs. Johnson. Or Cal vs. Josh. The two aspiring sports columnists shared traits with their Seattle heroes of yesteryear. Cal had heard this little pep talk from Josh before. He knew it was true, but he couldn't change his immediate situation, which served as an annoying reminder as to whose career path was already on a better trajectory. It was such a long-standing exchange between the two of them that even though not fully awake, Cal was firing back a salvo to Josh's slight air of superiority.

"Look. Just because you're miserable stuck in big city traffic and heading to your second job as a barista doesn't mean you have to rob me of the little joy I do have working in this virtual ghost town. Besides, maybe I like it here."

"Well, I'm going to find out for myself this weekend. You better show me the finest time that can be had in that cow town. I'm holding you to it."

"OK, OK. I'll make sure you have plenty of things to do. I'll never hear the end of it if you don't rule Statenville by the end of the weekend."

"All right. Looking forward to it. See you then, bro."

Cal hung up and rolled over. He had dreamed of covering the Mariners baseball team for the *Seattle Times*, but a general assignment reporter for *The Register* in Statenville, Idaho was the only job he could land. What self-respecting person would actually believe that working in Statenville would be a step toward a better job? Cal had no choice.

Cal valued his friendship with Josh, but a twinge of jealousy remained after Josh won the lone internship job at *The Times'* sports department straight out of college. More than three dozen college graduates hoping to become the next Mitch Albom applied—Josh somehow emerged victorious.

I hope he enjoys his day stuck in traffic and reformatting Formula One racing agate tonight. It wasn't a sincere hope, but in a moment of personal reflection, Cal admitted that the sting of his best friend from college beating him out for that job still smarted more than he wished. And with this thought, he pulled the covers over his head and attempted to fall back asleep.

The phone buzzed again.

"What now?" Cal shouted from his cover cave.

Emerging again into the light he discovered his editor's name dancing across his phone's window. *What does Guy want this early on a Monday?*

"Morning, Guy." Cal did his best to hide his irritation.

"Cal, get up and get dressed – and get down here right now! We've got a double murder in Statenville!"

"A double WHAT? Who?"

"Cody Murray and Riley Gold. I'll fill you in once you get here."

Guy hung up abruptly. Cal rubbed his eyes and began trying to imagine the circumstances for a double murder in Statenville.

Ha! Take that Josh! I'll bet there won't be any double murders for you to write about while stuck on the agate desk tonight!

Cal was wide awake now.

CHAPTER 3

IN THE FIVE MINUTES it took Cal to shower and towel dry his moppy dishwater blond hair, he tried to imagine what could have happened to two of Statenville's best football players. It didn't take long before he dumped thinking about the cause of the murders and began fantasizing over receiving a Pulitzer for his award-winning coverage of the mysterious Statenville serial killer.

Known for his trademark tardiness and sloppy appearance, Cal wasn't interested in propagating any false ideas that he was big time and the people of Statenville weren't. If anything, Josh was right – Cal needed motivation. He really wanted to be big time, but he was too depressed at the disappointing direction journalism had taken him. Writing for a weekly was never in his plans, but that is what he had been doing for almost a year now, pounding out articles on garden club meetings and school board decisions. He wanted to be writing about pro athletes and NFL lockouts. This was like being a superstar on the worst team in the league – what's the point?

Cal gave up on trying to impress anyone in Statenville. The townspeople held such a low image of The Register reporters that it didn't matter what he wore. If it doesn't matter, why not be comfortable. But wearing a tie on any day other than Sunday resulted in an endless line of questioning, such as, "What's the special occasion?" or "You sure do look nice. What's her name?"

But today felt different for Cal. *A double murder is a serious story and I need to be more serious looking.*

He dug some wrinkled khaki slacks out of his closet and paired it with a blue and green plaid oxford shirt. No tie. No one would confuse him for a Gap model, but he appeared more professional than on most days, which was Cal's meager goal as he raced out of his rundown duplex apartment door. *This could be big.*

On this late summer morning, Cal rushed to his black and maroon Civic . He engaged the engine and pressed the accelerator to the floor. A few seconds passed before Cal coaxed the engine underneath the replacement hood to life. He peeled onto Highway 278 for his five-minute commute. There was no time to waste if he was going to turn out a story sure to land at the top of the heap in his skimpy clips file.

As Cal slowed to a stop at an intersection, his iPhone buzzed again.

Kelly Mendoza's picture and name consumed the phone's screen.

Cal's mood momentarily changed from frenetic to giddy. If there was a good reason for staying in Statenville, it was Kelly Mendoza. Her fiery spirit overtook her common sense at times, but Cal dug spunk in a woman. It didn't hurt that Kelly possessed good looks either. A 5-foot-9 leggy firecracker with wavy shoulder-length brown hair and piercing blue eyes made for an intriguing package. Kelly embraced her Basque bloodlines in both spirit and beauty. Cal spent more time dreaming about asking her out than he did of covering the Mariners and the Seahawks combined. But there was that bothersome unwritten "no dating fellow employees" policy.

Cal pressed talk.

"Hey, Kelly. Happy Monday morning to you."

"Cal, I'm sure you heard the news ..."

"What news?" Cal said, playing coy.

"Guy hasn't called you yet?" Kelly asked.

"Yeah, yeah. He told me about the murders. I'm on my way into the office now." Cal could tell flirting wasn't a good idea.

"Well, I heard there's a serial killer on the loose," she said in a near-whisper. "Why would anyone want to target those two kids? There's got to be something else going on."

"Don't get too freaked out, OK? I'm sure there's a reasonable explanation for all of this." Cal just couldn't think of a plausible one at the moment to soothe Kelly's nerves.

"Are you packing any heat?"

"Packing what?" A grin spread across Cal's face.

"You got a gun?"

"Heck, no. What do you think this is? Dodge City? ... Are you?"

"You better believe it. I've got my Glock 21 within arm's reach."

Cal shuddered but responded with a nervous laugh at the thought of some poor criminal getting on the wrong end of Kelly's gun.

"Well, maybe I should ride with you today. You're the photographer on call today, aren't you?"

"Of course, Cal. I'm the only photographer ever on call."

"I know but it sounded like something you would say if you were working at a big city paper. We might be writing for a small town paper, but we've got a big city murder to cover now."

"I'm a little scared, but a tiny bit excited too," Kelly admitted.

"Ditto on both of those for me, too. See you at the office in a few." He ended the call.

What was going on? Cal wondered. *Is there really a serial killer on the loose in Statenville? And if so, why would he kill those two boys? Whatever could they have done? What could they have been involved with to deserve death?*

The paper's readers would likely be asking those same questions. It seemed like a good place to start when interviewing the local authorities. He imagined their answers and began to write the story in his mind.

He looked down Main Street at Statenville's usual brisk economic activity. Shoppers and business owners, many whom he knew, went about business as usual. He wondered if they knew a killer was on the loose. And in this small town, he wondered how they couldn't. Then he wondered why no one seemed scared.

CHAPTER 4

WHEN CAL WALKED THROUGH *The Register's* glass doors and into the newsroom, his eyes focused on Guy. Cal's curmudgeon editor stood on the other side of his desk, testing the length of his phone chord as he leaned out his door and snapped for a pen and pad from his assistant. Guy scratched down information that the caller relayed to him before hanging up the phone. He ran his hands through the thinning unkempt hair on his 62-year-old dome, as he exhaled a big breath. Then he spotted Cal.

"Get in here, Cal. You've got work to do!" he bellowed.

Cal then realized he was still standing outside the newsroom. He quickly moved toward his editor as he watched the veteran newsman come to life.

"Coming, boss!"

Cal's desk was on the second row of four in *The Register's* cramped newsroom. He sat behind Edith Caraway, the chipper receptionist who didn't try to hide her vintage era with the bouffant hairstyle she sported. Next to her was Earl Munroe, the middle-aged obituary and typesetter extraordinaire. Earl enjoyed sharing his mock obituaries almost as much as Edith enjoyed hearing them. Both had worked at the paper for more than 20 years and neither seemed to aspire to anything more.

Directly next to Cal's desk was copy editor and sole page designer, Terry Alford, armed with every technological advancement known to a modern newsroom. When he wasn't designing pages he spent most of his time flaunting his software and hardware superiority over the plebe reporters. His high-powered Mac desktop versus the reporters' aging Dell laptops was like comparing a Bazooka to a pea shooter – at least in his mind. He often exploded into diatribes about his virtual world conquests that would make Charlie Sheen blush. This usually produced exaggerated eye rolls and snickers from anyone unlucky enough to be caught in one of his technological barrages.

Behind Cal's desk was Kelly's workstation, the almighty photo department, and a spot for Sammy Mendoza, Kelly's 26-year-old cousin assigned to cover society functions who spent most of his time basking in nepotism. Sammy wasn't interested in small talk unless it included the latest gossip on who was running around on whom or who had purchased the latest top-of-the-line luxury automobile.

That left Guy and his secretary, Mindy Nicholson. Mindy didn't belong in this position. She was sharp, savvy and ambitious. But those things don't matter much when you decide to marry a sheep farmer. She would do anything for Guy and was exactly what he needed to maintain his sanity when something went awry.

Guy managed to cordon himself off from everyone else, if ever so slightly, with four-foot bluish-gray cubicle walls that were well past their prime. Mostly, it made Guy look silly as he tried to maintain some semblance of past newsroom glory as the editor of the Salt Lake City *Tribune*. But he pretended not to care that it looked just like you would imagine a small town newspaper in the middle-of-nowhere Idaho would look like.

Cal's desk, a relic rivaling Edith, was awash in papers. If Cal had 30 seconds to locate a meaningful piece of information on his desk or he would be typing in obituaries for a week, Earl would have been assured a week of vacation.

Normally on a Monday morning, only Edith and Earl would be at their posts, but today, there wasn't an empty seat – not even Sammy's.

Cal dumped his laptop bag on his desk and headed for Guy's space.

"So, what's the scoop, boss?"

"That's why I hire reporters, Cal," Guy growled. "They're supposed to bring me the scoop."

Cal sucked in a short breath. He was unsure of how to respond to Guy's thinly veiled accusation. But he didn't have a chance to say anything as Guy began barking instructions.

"Go to the sheriff's office and see if Jones will give you anything. Then report back to me and we'll figure out where to go next."

"You got it."

"And, Cal, be careful, you hear me? I want Kelly with you at all times to get some good art. We need a good dominant photo for Wednesday's paper. Even if it's Jones looking forlorn, I want *something.*"

"Will do, boss."

Kelly was already gathering her camera bag and notepad before Cal turned around and headed for his desk. She was waiting for Cal by the glass doorway as he scooped up his belongings.

Just as Cal was about to pass Edith near the front of the newsroom, she hung up the phone and began shaking.

"Cal, don't go anywhere," she said. "I think you're going to want to hear this."

Then she turned toward the back of the newsroom and utilized her Edithcom.

"Guy, there's been another murder!"

CHAPTER 5

THE JOINT CONSOLIDATION OF the Statenville Police Department with the Brooks County Sheriff's Department was the mastermind of Mayor Nathan Gold. Twelve years ago when he first assumed office in the town without term limits, the word "recession" was rarely uttered, much less the basis for decision-making among local, state and federal governments. But Gold looked like a genius over a decade later. Some called him visionary. Others considered him controlling, which certainly was a by-product of a city-county law enforcement department.

Nevertheless, the consolidation of resources and elimination of needless officers in a town where most people chose to remain in accordance with the law made Gold popular. Under his careful watch, Statenville had thrived – even in the midst of a down economy. Who could argue with his decisions when Statenville's major export business – Cloverdale Industries – was turning the city into a boon town, while neighboring cities in other counties were struggling to survive?

While there was still some debate among locals over the reasons for such a move, Sheriff Hunter Jones wasn't complaining. He enjoyed having more assets and control.

When Cal and Kelly burst through the Brooks County Sheriff's Office, located three storefronts down from the *Register*, Sheriff Jones didn't flinch. He sat with his dull black boots propped on his desk while giving a wooden toothpick a good workout between his teeth.

Jones deliberately looked the reporters up and down before speaking.

"Soooo, what brings you two cub reporters to my office this early on a Monday morning?" he asked as he leaked a wry smile.

"Sheriff Jones, you know good and well why we're here," Cal shot back, more than willing to dispense with any unnecessary pleasantries.

"You must've heard about the drug overdoses," Jones said, pausing for effect before continuing. "What a shame. I can't believe those boys threw away all that talent for a meth high."

Cal and Kelly looked at one another, both exhaling and relaxing for the first time since they heard the initial report.

"You mean, this isn't some vendetta murder or the work of some serial killer?" Cal asked, secretly hoping that his dreams of a Pulitzer weren't going to disappear due to simple drug usage.

"Do you think I'd still be here if that were true?" Jones fired back. He stood up and began moving toward the office coffee maker located on the vacant receptionist's desk in front of Cal and Kelly.

"Help yourself to the coffee," Jones offered, refilling his coffee mug and waiting for the duo to reply. While the Sherriff returned to his desk, both reporters eyed the small Styrofoam cups next to the dingy coffee pot, then declined the Sherriff's generous offer.

"What about the third murder victim? Who was he?" Cal asked.

"That would be Jim Reid's boy, Devin. And why do you keep using the 'M' word? They all died of a simple drug overdose."

"In a 24-hour period? Doesn't that seem a bit suspicious to you?" Cal questioned again.

"Well, sure it does. But that's why we investigate, little cubbie. Suspicion alone never gets a conviction. We need evidence. And we seem to have it."

Kelly grew tired of listening to Jones dance around the facts.

"You've got to give us more than that," she demanded.

"Well, what do you want to know? I think we all know that we need to be sensitive first and foremost to the families of the deceased. We don't need to make these boys look like a bunch of drug addicts."

It was obvious that Jones wasn't sincerely interested in answering any real questions. But neither Cal nor Kelly protested. The paper adhered to unspoken small town rules such as these.

"What kind of drugs were they using?" Kelly asked, unable to maintain the apparent soft gag order that was being issued by Jones.

"Well, we won't know that until the tox reports come back from Boise. But we found meth at all three scenes."

Jones ascribed to an age-old law enforcement trick: If you're forthcoming about an unusable piece of information, it could stem the tide of uncomfortable questioning. Or at the least it could keep you from appearing like a total jerk when you flat refused to answer a question deemed too invasive. He drummed his fingers on his desk as Cal and Kelly both began scribbling down details in their notebooks.

"But we won't know anything officially for at least two weeks," he said, negating what seemed like a juicy fact seconds ago.

"Got any reports yet?" Cal asked, eyeing two completed forms on the receptionist's desk.

"Nope," Jones lied. "Mercer and Dawkins will be back with full reports later this afternoon. They're still bagging evidence at the Reid place. You can talk to them here, later."

Jones' last sentence was an oblique order. Cal understood Jones didn't want them snooping around the Reid's house and he certainly didn't want them talking to his deputies before he got a chance to filter their conclusions. He wanted to maintain control of the situation.

Kelly saw it as a dare.

"OK, then. Just let us know if you hear anything else," Cal said as he and Kelly turned to leave.

"Will do."

Cal looked back over his shoulder and noticed Jones had plastered himself up against the window, watching them. Cal figured Jones wanted to make sure they didn't get in a car and head straight for the Reid place.

Kelly pulled Cal close, making him forget for a moment that Jones seemed overly interested in making sure this story remained low key.

"I'm parked out back," she whispered. They both were thinking the same thing.

CHAPTER 6

KELLY'S RED 2010 DODGE Charger engine roared as they pulled out of *The Register's* back alley parking lot and onto an adjacent side street, far out of the view of Jones' watchful eyes. She rolled down both front windows. Her face was stuck in a frown but she said nothing.

Cal's mind raced as he began mentally organizing the few facts he had. He would have preferred to soak in the glorious sun-kissed morning and the bonus that he was cruising around with Kelly. But today was not the day for flirtatious vibes. Three star athletes were dead in Statenville. Three *teenagers*. And Sheriff Jones, who said they all overdosed, seemed more intent on hiding something than revealing evidence that would confirm his simple drug overdose hypothesis.

After a minute of silence, Kelly broke the growing sense of apprehension both reporters were feeling.

"You know, this isn't going to be easy."

"Yeah, small town rules. People don't like you poking your nose in their business—especially when it's their dirty business."

"That Sheriff Jones is a lyin' dirt bag. He's unreported more criminal activity than there are cows at Buttercup Farms."

Cal tried to hide a smile. Kelly's metaphor was awkward and certainly one he would never use, but she never claimed to be a wordsmith. Yet with over 2,000 cows getting milked daily at Buttercup

Farms, Cal got her point: Jones was dirty.

"Don't you think everybody in this town is sketchy, Kelly?"

Kelly pursed her lips and slowly shook her head.

"This town is crawling with corruption. I can just feel it. And as much as I want to get out of this place, I can't wait to take over *The Register* and start turning over every rock until all these corrupt big shots are behind bars."

Cal knew Kelly had a gift for reporting, which made him wonder why she ever picked up a camera in the first place. He also didn't doubt Kelly would one day take over *The Register*, an action he would prevent if he could. It might be a blood bath, but Kelly would welcome the fight. *The Register* had been in her family for years and was currently published by Joseph Mendoza, her uncle and Sammy's father. If Uncle Joe cared about *The Register* being a thriving business enterprise in Statenville for years to come, he would turn it over to Kelly. However, he could conceivably give it to Sammy if his son ever found a way to motivate himself to do more in life than chase skirts and guzzle beer along the banks of the Snake River. Her future seemed uncertain and Cal selfishly rooted for Sammy, knowing he would be long gone from Statenville by then and hoping he might be able to lure Kelly away for a big city adventure.

For the next two minutes, Cal fidgeted with his digital voice recorder and snuck glances at Kelly while the two sped along a two-lane road leading east out of Statenville. Her shiny thick hair bounced in and out of the car as she looked straight ahead with her wire-rimmed Raybans. Cal knew he needed to focus but struggled to do so.

Kelly helped him get his mind back on the case.

"Have you ever been to the Reid place?" she asked.

"Nope. Anything special?"

"I've been out here a few times for social functions. My dad used to go hunting with Mr. Reid so we came out here a few times for cookouts. I think it's a nice place. But there it is. Judge for yourself."

Kelly took her right hand off the steering wheel and pointed to the one o'clock position. She was about two hundred yards away from the driveway leading to the Reid house, which sat about a quarter of a mile off the road on a ridge overlooking the Snake River. It was a sprawling brick ranch that made up for a lack of elegant craftsmanship with its sheer size. From Cal's perspective, the house seemed to stretch in all directions and defy the notion that public school teachers were paid a pauper's wage.

As Kelly turned into the Reid's lengthy dirt driveway and headed up the ridge toward the house, Cal noticed a sizable vegetable garden and a hay shed, harboring bales for a yet unseen herd of cattle or horses. However, Cal's interest in observing the Reid's property vanished once he saw the Brooks County Sheriff's deputy squad cars.

Cal could see Elliott Mercer taking notes as he interviewed Mr. Reid, the head of the two-person math department at Statenville High. Mrs. Reid, the other half of the Statenville High math department, buried her head in her hands and heaved tears as the Reid's 11-year-old daughter, Katie, consoled her. Jake Dawkins braced for their arrival. *This isn't going to be fun*, Cal thought.

Kelly eased her Charger into a parking pad a few feet from the house and a few yards from the squad cars and the Reids. Kelly and Cal both got out of the car and began walking toward the house. But Dawkins appeared determined to squash this impending inquisition, and was now striding toward them.

As the chief deputy and the most experienced law enforcement agent in Statenville, aside from Sheriff Jones, Dawkins knew diplomacy. Mercer's five years of experience in Statenville amounted to nothing in real world experience, though he had an impressive resume in private security before entering authentic law enforcement. Kelly figured if she batted her eyelashes at Mercer, he would likely reveal all the state's secrets. Mercer was professional but seemed willing to trade information given the right circumstances. Then there was Dawkins, the 12-year no-nonsense veteran of the sheriff's department who was all Cal and Kelly could handle.

For the second time that morning, a member of the Brooks County Sheriff's Department saw exchanging pleasantries with Cal and Kelly as a waste of time.

"There's nothing to see here. You two just need to turn around and go back to your office," Dawkins said, motioning them back with both his arms.

Kelly protested.

"Dawkins, you can't tell us to leave. We have just as much of a right as you do to question them...if they want to talk to us."

She knew her assertion was wrong, but she wanted to let Dawkins know that they weren't going anywhere.

"Wrong, Miss Mendoza," Dawkins fired back. "I'm in charge when it's a crime scene."

CHAPTER 7

"CRIME SCENE?" CAL AND Kelly both asked in unison, suddenly confused again about the real nature of what happened in Statenville over the past 24 hours.

"You heard me. Now get back in your car and get on out of here," Dawkins growled.

Kelly's gusto was rubbing off on Cal. He stood his ground.

"Dawkins, this morning Jones told us that all three deaths in the past 24 hours were drug overdoses. Now, that's not exactly a crime scene."

Dawkins backpedaled.

"Well, we think it's a drug overdose but we're still collecting evidence."

"So, what have you found that makes you think this could be something else?"

"Cal, Kelly, I think it's best that you go now. You don't want to make a scene in front of this grieving family, do you?"

Cal and Kelly shot knowing glances at one another. This was not a hill to die on. Not today. Not with Mrs. Reid grieving the loss of her son. Not with Dawkins channeling his inner Steven Segal. Not with two other "crime scenes" that had no officers present.

The pair didn't say a word as they turned and headed straight for Kelly's car.

"Who does he think he is?" asked Kelly as she twisted the ignition.

"That Dawkins is such a punk. There's obviously a lot more going on here than he's telling us."

As Kelly's car roared back down the road, she bit her lip and shook her head, muttering hollow threats about Dawkins and his job and what her next column would be about if she had one. Cal slunk in his seat, flummoxed over the Brooks County Sheriff's Department stonewall. He peered in his side mirror as the scene shrunk from sight.

Cal noticed Dawkins immediately began talking into the radio mic attached to his upper sleeve. *Who could he be calling?* Cal wondered. *Are we being watched?* His eyes remained fixed on Dawkins.

Dawkins then looked up and glared in the direction of Kelly's car, which was beginning to turn onto the highway. Cal shuddered. Dawkins' haunting stare seemed more than passing interest about where the pair was headed next. Cal's firm belief that the Brooks County Sheriff's Department was just a notch above a living Mayberry – complete with Don Knotts as the sheriff and Gomer Pyle as his chief deputy – was being shaken. Gone was Dawkins' happy-go-lucky disposition. Dawkins' mouth said one thing, but his body language said something else, a something else that made Cal quake with fear.

Kelly made it to the highway and turned right, heading toward the Murray's house.

Cal looked back toward the Reid house again only to see Dawkins still speaking into his radio and keeping his eyes locked on Kelly's car. More than likely, Cal thought Dawkins was telling someone where they were headed and to watch out for them.

Finally, Cal broke the silence. "What have we got ourselves into, Kelly?"

"I don't know, but this smells like some sort of cover up." She jammed her foot on the gas pedal and Dawkins vanished from sight.

CHAPTER 8

WHEN CAL AND KELLY returned to *The Register*, they found Guy had retired his "I'm the Boss" coffee cup with a drink more appropriate for the afternoon. Guy was sipping from one of those giant plastic cups from the Flying J filled to the brim with soda when he noticed the pair return to the office.

"There you two are! Get back to my office right now," Guy yelled.

Cal didn't bother setting down his bag at his desk. He knew Guy was on a rare – but trademark – rampage. Cal had observed that Guy only exhibited this behavior when there was a real news story taking place. The events of the past 24 hours certainly qualified as real news, especially in Statenville.

With two chairs across from Guy's desk, Kelly took the seat closest to the cubicle doorway. Cal squeezed past her and into the seat wedged against the wall. They were both barely in their seats before Guy commenced.

"What have you two been up to?" he demanded. "On your account, I've taken two cautionary phone calls from Sheriff Jones and been called into Joseph's office – and it's not even noon!"

"I can explain –" Cal started.

"You better start talking fast. I don't have time for nuanced excuses."

"We started by going to talk with Sheriff Jones, and he started giving us the run around along with a suggestion to more or less drop it," Cal answered.

"A suggestion? Like, 'Stop digging. No one will like what you find'?"

"Yeah, kind of like that."

"And so you had to go keep digging, of course."

"Boss, isn't that what we're supposed to do? I'm telling you, something strange is going on and people will want to know about it."

"According to Joseph and Hunter Jones, nobody in this town wants to know about anything other than funeral arrangements and where to send flowers for these poor boys' families."

"And you're buying that?"

"I don't know what I'm buying yet, but I don't like anything that gets the publisher and the sheriff crawling all over me. You got it?" The stressed-out editor pointed his index finger at the two as if it were a pistol.

Kelly nodded her head, but Cal knew she had no intention of halting her investigation. Neither did he. Cal continued his protest.

"So how are we supposed to do our jobs?"

"Figure it out, cubbie. But do it without having my boss and the law put the squeeze on me. Now get out of here and let me know when you have something."

Kelly got up and headed for her desk. Cal didn't move.

"What makes you think we don't already have something of interest?"

"You don't. Now get out of here before you ruin the five precious minutes I have left of this morning."

Cal huffed as he returned to his desk and began organizing his notes.

"Have you ever heard the saying, 'Discretion is the better part of valor'?" whispered a voice in Cal's ear.

Cal turned to see a smart-aleck grin spread across Kelly's face.

"I think I know who is behind all this, Cal. Let's go talk about it over lunch."

Cal grabbed his briefcase and ignored the rest of the newsroom employees. For the second time today, he was invited to ride in

Kelly's car. Guy's tirade withstanding, it was turning out to be a pretty good day for Cal.

Law enforcement feathers ruffled? Check. Big breaking story with potential for an award-winning article? Check. Business or not, riding with Kelly in her sports car? Check. Lunch with Kelly at Ray-Ray's? Near perfection. And it was only noon.

CHAPTER 9

CAL'S BREAKFAST IN HIS frantic rush to get to the office ended up being two untoasted pop tarts and a cup of coffee. It was hardly the breakfast of champions, but most definitely a staple for reporters. By lunchtime, Cal needed something more substantial. He needed brain food. He needed Ray-Ray's.

Ray-Ray's was the best – and only – barbecue joint in all of Brooks County. Prior to Ray-Ray's, the only barbecue to be found there was the processed kind found in the refrigerated section of a grocery store. But six months ago, brothers William and Burt Ray from Arkansas relocated to Statenville and opened up one of the best barbecue restaurants in the state. Within three months, Ray-Ray's word-of-mouth reputation was so strong that a food critic from the Boise newspaper made the two-and-a-half hour drive to Statenville resulting in a glowing review. After that, Ray-Ray's needed no more help in attracting customers.

Cal and Kelly inhaled the smell of a hickory wood grill and spicy barbecue sauce as they opened the restaurant door. Nothing could change Cal's mood like the aroma of barbecue, nothing other than eating it, that is. They both placed their order and then found a table outside to reduce the number of nosy ears.

"So, Kelly, who do you think is behind all of this?" asked Cal, who, after one bite of ribs, had already managed to get a thick stream of barbecue sauce oozing down the center of his chin.

"Well, I don't know if someone left it on my desk as a hint or if it's just by pure coincidence, but when I sat down at my desk, I had a paper folded to this headline."

Kelly pulled a two-week old copy of *The Register* out of her purse. It was folded so that only one headline was showing.

"BOISE DEVELOPER, CITY CLASH"

Cal kept eating as he scanned the article written by Guy two weeks ago; an article he missed while covering the end of the summer city softball league tournament. The article painted the scene of Statenville's contentious city council meeting over the re-zoning of a particular property owned by Boise developer, BCH Homes. It was currently zoned as agricultural land, but BCH wanted to build a 100-home subdivision to accommodate the city's growth. There was rumor that a new pulpwood plant was going to be relocating to Statenville within the next 18 months – and BCH saw this as an opportunity to build plenty of new homes. The article quoted a handful of local men and women upset about the potential re-zoning and what it would do to their property values. Standard reporting.

Cal didn't see the connection to the three dead teens.

"I'm not sure I get it," Cal answered after re-reading the article.

"Let me help you out, Einstein." Kelly took the paper from Cal and circled three names with a pen: Murray, Reid, and Gold. The three last names of the teens who were now dead. She handed the paper back to Cal. "Now, do you get it?"

"Well, there's at least two other people quoted in the article and nobody in their family died. Besides, do you really think that a developer would hire someone to kill the sons of three people who spoke out at a meeting? If you're that sinister, why not put the squeeze on the commissioners themselves?"

Kelly went on a mini-tirade that reminded Cal of her Uncle Joe.

"Look, we've got nothing right now, but this is as plausible as anything – and you just want to dismiss it like it's nothing and that people aren't really that evil? Well, let me tell you something, Mr. Outsider. You have no idea the havoc outside development has wreaked on this town! I will be shocked if this isn't who's behind all this."

Cal motioned for Kelly to settle down, nearing embarrassment at the scene she was causing. He sucked the barbecue sauce off every finger, using the stall tactic as an opportunity to carefully choose his response.

He leaned across the table and spoke in a low, calm voice in hopes of tempering Kelly's excitement.

"Look, I know I don't know all of Statenville's past history, but you're not thinking with your head – you're thinking with your heart. Past experience doesn't always dictate future actions. However, if you want to warn those people quoted in the story, I'm fine with that."

Kelly looked down and shook her head as she cooled off.

"All I'm saying, Cal, is that's the *least* we can do. If they are next and we don't say anything, we might both regret it. And that's not something I want to live with."

"OK, let's make some calls."

The two crammed down the remaining ribs and French fries and headed back to the newsroom.

* * *

Neither Cal nor Kelly noticed the black Ford F-250 parked at the end of the block.

As Kelly turned onto the road and headed back to the office, the black truck eased onto the road behind her.

CHAPTER 10

GUY WAS STANDING AT Edith's desk when Cal and Kelly returned from lunch.

"So, did my two least favorite gumshoes crack this case?" Guy demanded.

Cal looked at the mug Guy clutched with both hands. He wondered just how many cups Guy had to get that cranky by lunchtime. "Uh, no, but Kelly has a theory?"

"A theory? What is this? *CSI?* We run a newspaper here. We deal in facts. What facts do you have that we can report in our paper without getting us sued, without getting me chewed out by the publisher, and without making Hunter Jones look like the fool that he is?"

In the course of 15 seconds, Kelly lost her confidence – and her courage.

"We've got nothing yet, but as soon as we do, I'll let you know," she said.

Guy muttered another biting comment about Cal and Kelly's intelligence and stormed back to his office.

Kelly looked sheepishly at Cal, who was boring a hole in her with his stare.

"What? What did you want me to say?"

"Look, let's each make a phone call to warn the other two people in the story and get back out there. I want to talk with a few people who might know something about these kids."

Cal returned to his desk and began dialing the number for Brady Perkins, the farmer who sold the land to BCH Homes. In Guy's article, Perkins complained that he thought he was selling the land to another farmer and argued that BCH Homes posed as a buyer under false pretenses. He also expressed his disappointment that precious Idaho topsoil would be covered with pavement.

From reading Brady's comments, Cal wasn't sure if the old farmer was sincere or simply trying to stave off the growing disdain locals felt toward him for selling the property to an outsider.

Brady picked up his phone.

"Hello?"

"Mr. Perkins?"

"Speaking."

"This is Cal Murphy from *The Register*. How are you today, sir?"

"Well, I'm happy with my subscription. Thank you very much. Now, I've got to get back to plowing."

"Wait, Mr. Perkins, I wasn't calling about your subscription."

"Is this a survey? Cause I don't have time for that either."

"No, Mr. Perkins. This isn't a survey. I just wanted to warn you that your life might be in danger."

"In danger? What in the world are you talking about?"

"Mr. Perkins, are you aware that three teenage boys have died in the last 24 hours and authorities suspect foul play?"

"Yeah, I heard. What's that got to do with me?"

"Well, sir, in some of our investigating, we discovered that in one of our articles each of those boys' parents lashed out against BCH Homes during the city council meeting a few weeks ago. And the same article quoted you."

"So what, you think I'm next?" Brady said in a mocking tone.

"Well, we don't know if there's a connection, but we thought we'd at least warn you and your family."

"What family? I've only got myself to look after. You don't need to worry about me. Me and my Smith and Wesson are pretty good at taking care of me."

"OK, Mr. Perkins. I wanted to give you a heads up just in case."

Click. The line went dead.

For a second, Cal wondered if Kelly's theory was right and maybe some cloak-and-dagger hit man had just offed Brady Perkins. But then he decided it was much more likely that Mr. Perkins simply hung up on a crazy reporter. Cal didn't give it another thought.

He spun around to watch Kelly hang up.

"So, did Mrs. Washburn sound concerned?"

Kelly rolled her eyes. "No. She laughed at me and said she didn't have teenage boys. Then she started telling me the rumor she heard about how the boys died."

"I'll bet that was interesting."

"Yeah, it actually was quite entertaining. She said the prevailing rumor is that a deranged mountain lion wandered down from the Sawtooths and mauled those three boys. And it's still roaming around Brooks County looking for its next victim."

Cal started chuckling at Mrs. Washburn's theory and the idea that a mountain lion could roam freely in any Idaho town for more than 10 minutes without getting put down by a high-powered rifle.

"What about Mr. Perkins? What did he say?"

"He said he wasn't concerned – and then he hung up on me."

"Nice."

"OK, so you ready to hit the road again?"

"Sure. Where to now, Sherlock?"

"Statenville High School. Coach Mike Miller's office."

CHAPTER 11

MIKE MILLER'S OFFICE WOULD have made Cal's favorite TV detective, Monk, go into shock.

Crusty half-eaten sandwiches were wedged next to mounds of paperwork on his desk, some that appeared classroom related, others that looked like football plays. Two pens with chewed off ends oozed ink onto his desk. Phys Ed text books were piled in the corner next to used mouth pieces and broken helmets. The white cinder block walls remained bare with the exception of a cheaply framed 1994 District Coach of the Year certificate hanging slightly off kilter. A wafting aroma of sweaty gym socks and tobacco juice hung in the air.

After a year of covering the Statenville Wildcats football program, Cal had never met Miller in his office. Now he knew why. He wondered if a hazmat suit was more appropriate attire for this unannounced visit.

Miller wasn't in his office.

"Can I help you?" came a voice from behind Cal and Kelly.

Cal spun around to see Buddy Walker, the head boys basketball coach and an assistant football coach.

Walker was new by Statenville standards, set to enter his third year at the school. Coaching jobs rarely opened up at Statenville High. It was so far off the beaten path that nobody considered it a stepping-stone for his coaching career—it was a final destination.

You didn't go to Statenville High if you wanted to coach in Boise or Salt Lake. You went there because you were either from there or you wanted to live there until you died. Walker certainly wasn't the former, but many of the townspeople weren't convinced he was the latter either. Walker wasn't the smartest coach by Cal's estimation. But he possessed plenty of youthful energy, a valuable trait Walker needed when he was hired to replace his popular predecessor Nick Zentz, who died in a tragic hunting accident.

"Hi, Coach Walker. How are you?"

"Oh, hey there, Cal. We could be doing a lot better today."

"Yeah, I'm still in shock that those three boys are gone. I interviewed Cody last week for our football preview."

Walker looked down and dragged a used mouthpiece across the floor with his foot. His face silently agreed with Cal.

"How's Coach Miller holding up?" Kelly asked.

"He's doing all right under the circumstances. But he's pretty torn up. This team is like a family and right now we're all hurting."

"Is Coach Miller here?" Kelly asked.

"Yeah, you can find him in his own private sanctuary—the football field."

Up until this moment, the report of the three boys' death was just a sensational news story. Now, the human element of what happened struck Cal. He began to feel a little uncomfortable, even embarrassed that he hadn't thought of how Miller might be feeling. But he still had a job to do no matter how awkward it was.

"Thanks, Buddy," Cal said somberly.

Cal and Kelly quietly exited Miller's office and headed for the football field.

Statenville High may play eight-man football and have only 3,500 people living in the city limits, but Wildcat Stadium had a seat for every one of them.

Cal often wondered why. When it came to wins and losses, the whole athletic program was an embarrassment. But that didn't seem to matter to the people of Statenville. They supported their team no matter what. And if you didn't believe that, the fact that Miller had two winning seasons in 20 years – and about to begin his 21st – was proof enough.

Cal figured the death of three team members would be devastating to Miller under any circumstances. It was hard enough to find enough boys to suit up each season. In a tragic 24-hour period, his roster had been reduced to 14 players. But *these* three boys were supposed to lead Statenville to a district crown and maybe even a state title. That only added to an already difficult professional situation for Miller.

When Cal and Kelly reached the stadium, they found Miller sitting in the bleachers at the 50-yard line, staring blankly at the field.

"Cody had a good shot to start at Washington State next year," Miller said without even looking at the reporters. "Those boys had their whole lives in front of them. I can't believe they threw it all away for drugs."

"It does seem a little odd, doesn't it?" Cal responded.

"So, I guess you want some comments for your story."

"If you don't feel like talking right now, I understand. It's OK. We can come back later."

"Now is as good of a time as any."

"Coach, I guess the biggest mystery to me is why a kid with such a promising future would be doing drugs."

"What promising athlete isn't doing some type of drug today?" Miller's cynicism took Cal aback. He continued. "I know some of these boys do drugs, but nobody in this town seems to care. Not even the parents."

"Did you ever talk to Cody's parents about his drug usage?"

"Yeah, one time I saw Cody's dad after practice and I mentioned that he might be using. But his dad just laughed at me and said, 'If it helps him get ahead, I'm all for it.' It made me sick."

"Does meth really help you as an athlete?" Kelly interjected.

"I've heard it gives you a lot of energy. So for a guy who really wanted to make it out of Statenville as an athlete, it helped him work out longer. And the more you work out, the stronger you get and the more you can do physically. Heck, most college coaches don't care if you're smart as long as you look good gettin' off the bus, so where do you think an athlete who wants to play in college is going to spend his time? It ain't studying after school, that's for sure."

Miller's straight talk stunned Cal into silence. Coaches always had standard answers for his questions, but Miller was off script. It was refreshing – and shocking.

Kelly noticed Cal was entranced by Miller's honesty. She continued her line of questioning.

"So, how long did you know Cody was using?"

"It started last summer, probably just as a way to help him gain an edge in the weight room. But it wasn't too long before he was addicted. He impressed enough college coaches in the fall to get a handful of scholarship offers, but I didn't suspect he'd ever really make it to campus."

"That bad, huh?"

"Yeah, he was going south in a hurry. Physically, you couldn't tell. But mentally? He wasn't nearly as sharp as he was his sophomore year or even last season. I even considered moving him to running back so he wouldn't have to remember so much. But this town would've gone nuts. Even I would've lost my job over a coaching move like that."

Cal smiled. Miller might be grieving, but his sense of humor – and grip on reality – was intact. It was enough to break him out of his catatonic state.

"But isn't this unusual, Coach? I mean, three guys in 24 hours by using meth and all overdosed? I'm not a drug expert, but that seems highly improbable."

"So, you think it was the mountain lion that got them?"

Kelly and Cal shot glances at each other, recalling Mrs. Washburn's crazy rumor.

Kelly played dumb. "Mountain lion? What are you talking about?"

"You guys haven't heard that yet? I thought you were the reporters, not me."

"Where did you hear that?" asked Kelly, feigning surprise.

"Oh, it's just a rumor I heard, but somebody told me that they heard Cody and Devin's bodies looked like they had been mauled by a mountain lion. I don't know any drugs that will do that. I know it's a crazy rumor, but it might be something that the parents of those boys need right now to make sure they don't go crazy with feelings of regret, like they didn't pay enough attention to their sons."

"According to you, they didn't."

"Look, I'm just processing this stuff out loud with you two, but can I trust you not to report anything I've said?"

Cal sighed. He had been capturing the whole conversation on his digital recorder. He hit the stop button.

"OK, Coach. I promise not to attribute any of this information to you. But if this turns out to be something more suspicious, I might call you and ask for your permission to reveal some information as an unnamed source. Deal?"

"Only if there's a killer involved and it'll help catch him. I don't want to speak ill of the dead or the parents of the dead, especially in this town."

Cal stood up.

"Thanks for your time, Coach. And I'm really sorry for your loss. I know your job in the days ahead is going to be tough, but I'm sure you'll get through it."

"Thanks, Cal. Kelly. You two have a nice day."

Neither reporter spoke until they got into Kelly's car.

"A mountain lion?" Cal asked. "Are these people for real? Why would anyone think a mountain lion could kill three teens in three different places in a day's time?"

"I don't know, but there's only one way to find out."

"Yeah, good luck with that. Sheriff Jones won't give us a thing, much less an accurate coroner's report."

Kelly was already hitting high RPMs in second gear when she shifted into third and smiled.

"Did you forget that my cousin is the coroner?"

CHAPTER 12

GUY DRUMMED HIS FINGERS on his desk and contemplated what to do next. Three suspicious deaths in one day. That's the reason he left *The Tribune* seven years ago. He didn't want to bellow at reporters any more for getting scooped by Channel 4. He didn't want to teeter on the verge of a heart attack each day as he feared he might lose his job for some green reporter slipping a libelous comment into a 1A story. He didn't want to be hated by everyone who worked under him.

So he quit.

Yes, Statenville afforded Guy the opportunity to live out his days as a newspaperman in peace. Rotary Club dinners. Garden Club grip-and-grins. Mayoral elections. Anything beat daily crime and corruption.

But that was before Guy knew Statenville had a hallowed secret. He didn't actually know what it was – and he was paid handsomely not to search for it. Guy had a gentleman's agreement with the man he surmised was the mastermind. Every month Guy found a brown paper bag on his back porch full of $20 bills – 100 of them, to be exact. He knew because he counted it every time. Of course, Guy didn't have to go along when he was first approached. But the way the proposition was presented, Guy figured he had no choice. It was either take the money and pretend like this really was a sleepy little town or move to some other place and hope its secret was less toxic. The first option seemed the best, especially since he hadn't exactly amassed a sufficient nest egg for retirement. *Besides, could this secret really be that big of a deal?* Guy rationalized it away and didn't dwell on it much, especially since nothing worth digging into had ever come across his desk.

When certain whispers wafted Guy's way – the kind he begged for in Salt Lake – he acted hard of hearing. Some of the townspeople suspected he knew the secret, which is why they respected him all the more. He was becoming one of them, complicit in his silence. And for that, he was treated as one of their own.

But today, reality rocked Guy's fantasy. The truth was dying to get out. Literally.

Were these deaths tied to Statenville's dark secret? Perhaps. But would he reveal it, once the truth was known for certain? He didn't know for how much longer he could suppress his editor instincts, even if it meant giving up the cash – or something far worse.

His phone rang.

"This is Guy."

"Hey, Guy. Just wanted to find out how you're going to handle the big story this week," came the voice on the other end.

"With care and sensitivity."

"OK, just checking because I've seen two of your reporters out snooping around like they work for *The New York Times.* You keep an eye on them, you understand?"

"Don't worry. I've got them under control."

Guy lied and hung up. He knew that if he tried to sideline Cal and Kelly on this story, he might have a fight on his hands with his reporters. He would have to figure out something to appease everyone.

Guy then smiled as a good thought registered in his mind. *This might be easier than I thought.* Cal was diligent but he had never covered a story like this. And Kelly? Her uncle could handle her.

Of course, that is if they didn't find any damning evidence. One phone call could mitigate the situation, but not control it entirely.

He drummed his fingers on the desk again, resisting the urge to do what was right by all journalism ethics. It was like Dr. David Banner trying to restrain his inner Hulk.

***

Cal's iPhone buzzed, dancing on the console of Kelly's car.

"Hello, Boss?"

"Where are you?" demanded Guy.

"We're just leaving Statenville High. I went to talk with Coach Miller and get his reaction . . . see if he knew anything else about those kids."

"OK, well, get back here ASAP. We need to talk."

"Have you found out anything new?"

"Yeah, I have. I found out you've continued poking your nose in the wrong places today and nobody likes it."

"Just doing my job, boss."

"Your job is to write what I assign you. Now get back here so we can finish this conversation in person."

Click.

Cal knew Guy was cranky, but his boss's behavior was bordering on erratic and irrational.

"Does Guy seem a little off today?" Cal asked Kelly.

"When is he not a little off?"

"No, seriously. You don't find his behavior somewhat... strange, even for Guy?"

"Well, think about it, Cal. Guy moved here to get away from all this murder and mayhem. Now it's followed him to his own private Mayberry."

"True. But it seems like he's dealing with something else. I can't put my finger on it."

"Well, I wouldn't worry about it. To be honest, I can't believe more of the town isn't on edge and acting a little crazy after three teens die in a 24-hour period."

"I know, but something just doesn't seem right about him." Cal stared out the window at the distant mountains.

"You're thinking too much."

"Maybe I am, but he wants us back in the office ASAP."

Kelly laughed. "As soon as possible for me translates into after I've visited my cousin, the coroner."

"Ah, Kelly. I'm having more fun with you on this case today than I've had since I moved here."

She shot him a cautious look.

Cal shifted nervously in his seat.

"Cal, I swear if you're hitting on me during an investigative report of three murdered teens ..." Her voice trailed off.

Cal smiled and put his hands up as to say he was innocent. He then busied himself by silencing his phone, not wanting to be interrupted by Guy until they got back to the office.

* * *

The Ford F-250 continued to maintain a safe distance behind Kelly's car. The driver hit *1* on his cell phone's speed dial to file his report. "It appears they're headed back to the office," the driver said.

The man on the other end seemed pleased.

"Keep me posted if they make any unexpected stops. I don't want this turning into a big news story."

CHAPTER 13

KEVIN MENDOZA PUSHED THE dark-framed glasses back up his nose. He peered at his clipboard and then returned his gaze at the lifeless body of Cody Murray.

Nothing prepared him for investigating the deaths of three teenage boys in a 24-hour period. While attending the University of Washington Medical School, Kevin had seen a few gunshot wounds and one pit bull attack victim. But never a cadaver even close to what he was looking at now.

Despite the pervasive rumor around Statenville, none of the victim's wounds appeared to come from any variety of feline, mountain lion or otherwise. But they definitely looked like claw marks, scratch marks from someone in close proximity to each victim. Long slashes across their torso. Legs. Arms. Faces. No segment of the body was clear.

Kevin was nearly convinced it was a surprise attack of some kind, maybe even a vicious one that immediately sedated each victim before carving him up. Then he looked under their fingernails. That's when he realized that this was more freakish than he could have ever imagined.

He picked up Cody's hand and looked again. Scraped off skin was compacted under each fingernail. Kevin figured even his favorite TV medical examiner would have been perplexed by how such a death could have occurred.

Without more testing, he couldn't be certain; but Kevin's initial assessment was that each victim literally scratched himself to death. *Exsanguination* would be the term used in his official report, but it would be reported in the media as "bleeding to death." They scratched themselves with such fierceness and intensity that they severed several major arteries and bled to death.

Kevin was finishing up his preliminary report when his cell phone rang.

"Dr. Mendoza here."

"What did you find?" asked the voice on the other end.

"Who is this?"

"You know good and well who this is. Now answer my question: How did those boys die?"

Kevin paused, unsure of whether he wanted to reveal his initial findings, especially to this caller.

"I think they all bled to death."

"Nope. They overdosed on drugs."

"I beg your pardon. We won't know from the tox screens that they overdosed for a few more days. But that's not what ultimately killed them."

"I think you misunderstood me. I said, 'They overdosed on drugs.' And you're canceling the tox screens. You understand?"

"OK, got it."

Kevin wasn't thrilled to go along with this cover-up, but if he was going to be re-elected this fall, complying with his request made sense.

He hung up the phone and began filling out a new form. He slid his old report to the bottom of his clipboard, wanting to investigate on his own for curiosity's sake. He would present the fake report to the Sheriff's Department and media, but their deaths were too bizarre to not investigate.

Kevin then wrote a short email to the lab in Boise, canceling the tox screens of the victims' blood.

The cover-up was almost complete—and then he heard his cousin calling his name down the hall.

"Kevin?! Are you here?" Kelly shouted.

He knew she was working her way down the short hallway, looking for him in each room.

Kevin pulled sheets over two of the victims in his exam room. He shoved his clipboard out of sight and prepared to sell his cousin on the fact that he was leaving the room and should join him in his office.

Their hands both gripped the door knob on opposite sides at the same moment. Kelly let go. The door flew open and she was staring her cousin – Dr. Kevin Mendoza, the county coroner – in the eyes. They were eyes of guilt.

CHAPTER 14

CAL HAD DECIDED TO let Kelly take the lead on this final investigative stop before returning to *The Register's* office to face an irritable Guy. Kelly suggested he remain in the vehicle until she convinced her cousin to let them take a look at the bodies. But he was too impatient to wait for Kelly's signal, which may or may not come. Besides, all those mountain lion rumors made him want to squelch them by seeing the bodies with his own two eyes.

After Kelly disappeared into the coroner's office, Cal stepped out of the car and headed for the entrance.

He was 30 seconds behind Kelly as he slipped into the building that lacked a secretary or front desk attendant. Cal was just in time to see the door shut before the two disappeared into Kevin's office. He heard Kelly pleading with her cousin as he slipped past the door in the hall.

"Come on, Kevin. I won't take any pictures. Just let me look at the bodies." Kelly's plea filled the hallways.

"No, Kelly. I'll release my final report to the sheriff and you can obtain a copy from him."

Kevin's stonewall began to irritate Kelly. She paused and then went on the offensive.

"What are you hiding, Doctor Mendoza? I want to know!"

"I'm not hiding anything and you aren't authorized to be in there. Those bodies are evidence in an official law enforcement investigation."

"Oh, so it was a murder?"

"I never said that. I'm investigating what happened to these boys. Now, if you'll excuse me, I've still got a lot of paperwork to get to today before I can go home."

The doctor was forcing Kelly to take one step into the hallway. In the dimly lit hall Kelly could see Cal out of the corner of her eye standing in front of the door to the examination room. She immediately knew what the daring reporter was up to so she redoubled her efforts to keep Kevin in his office.

"Isn't there an election coming up soon?" Kelly asked.

Kelly knew how much he loved his job but how much he hated the campaigning portion of it. Kevin usually ran uncontested. But in the last election, Gerald Bachman made life uncomfortable for him. Bachman nearly pulled a stunning upset in a town where a Mendoza had served in the coroner's position for more than 50 years.

Kevin hesitated but refused to yield to Kelly's demand. She stepped back into his office and pressed him further.

"It'd be a shame for Bachman to come across a few photos that would give people the wrong idea about what you might do with their dead relatives."

Kevin froze. He stared at Kelly in horror. In the hall Cal worked feverishly to pick the lock to the exam room.

"I still have pictures from when you and some of your friends got drunk one Saturday night. Remember the night you came up with the brilliant idea to break into the morgue and take pictures of the sheriff's dead brother with a wig on, among other things"

"Seriously? You'd do that to me?"

"Yeah. You bet I would. Playing dress up with the sheriff's deceased brother may seem like hours of hilarity when you're 17. But when you're 32 and an elected city official, frolicking drunk in the morgue becomes a skeleton in your political closet – especially when the press knows about it."

Kelly let that last sentence hang in the air before making her point clear.

"My brother was with that crowd of Einsteins and just so happened to catch it all on his film. One night while rummaging through his keepsakes, I found some of those pictures from your juvenile humor. I kept a few of the snapshots and asked him about it one day. Let's just say, his recollections are far worse than the photos and would be the least of your concerns."

Kevin retreated slowly back to his desk. He supposed there was no way to thwart her threat – but he decided he would take his chances with her.

"Look, Kelly. You have no idea the amount of pressure I'm under. But losing an election pales in comparison to being dumped into Cold River Canyon by some goon. So, do what you've got to do, but I'm much more afraid for my life than I am from people seeing some embarrassing pictures of my teenage indiscretions printed in the paper."

Kevin hung his head low and plopped down in this chair He wasn't giving in to her demands.

***

The man in the F-250 lit a cigarette and took a long drag. He tapped the steering wheel and looked at his watch.

What is taking them so long?

The phone rang. It was the voice.

"Have they left yet?"

"Nope. They're still inside. What do you want me to do?"

"It seems like Cagney and Lacey need more than a simple scare. You know what to do."

The man smiled as he scrawled out a threatening note, thinking less about the note and more about the green light to do some damage.

CHAPTER 15

KELLY CONTINUED TO KEEP Kevin occupied with other unimportant matters, making a few more worthless pleas to let her see the bodies. Meanwhile, Cal wasted no time picking the lock to the exam room door. Cal was no thief, but his penchant for losing track of his dorm room keys while he was in college forced him to acquire this skill by studying YouTube videos. The door clicked open. As Cal slipped into the room, the biting smell of formaldehyde and other chemical cleaners overwhelmed him. Cal cringed and fought the urge to cough.

Cal looked at the tag on the body's toe. It read "Cody Murray." Not that Cal needed to read it. He had spent plenty of time in one-on-one interviews with Cody during football season – and baseball season, too. His face seemed immune to the disfigurement but his chiseled body was barely recognizable.

As Cal edged closer to the examination table, he gasped at Cody's body in its mutilated shape. The mountain lion rumor seemed unlikely when compared to the cuts and gashes etched deep into the quarterback's skin. If anyone who originated such a rumor had actually seen Cody's body in this state, Cal figured the rumor would have been more sensational, like the Statenville Sasquatch.

Long grooves one to two inches deep crisscrossed Cody's upper body. A simple swipe wasn't enough. The perpetrator's nails had to gouge a new rut in his skin.

On Cody's legs, the cuts were vertical.

"I can't imagine a drug overdose doing this to you," Cal said to Cody's dead body.

Cal spent a few more seconds inspecting the body, struggling to come up with any plausible theory. He pulled out his iPhone and began taking photos. Then he took some video. No one would believe it if the told them.

That's when he saw the remaining two bodies. He snapped more photos of their mangled torsos, unable to formulate any ideas as to what could have caused such an apparently painful death.

Cal quietly exited the room, careful not to tip off Kevin to the fact that someone had seen his precious bodies. Cal snuck out a side door and was sitting in Kelly's car when she came out the front door.

She climbed in and inserted her key in the ignition and stopped.

Before she could ask Cal about what information he gathered, a note stuck between her windshield and driver's side wiper flapped in the wind.

She got out of the car and grabbed the note. She shuddered as she read it.

Watch yourself ... or you might end up like those boys

"What is it?" Cal asked.

"Somebody doesn't like what we're doing."

"They need to take a number."

"But this is a threat, Cal."

"Let me see that." Cal grabbed the note, read it, and handed it back to Kelly. "I get threats all the time. Nothing ever happens. Somebody is trying to intimidate us to stop. If they want to stop us, there's only one way."

"Well, you must've seen something in there that convinced you it's worth the risk. What did you see?"

"I have no idea. I've never seen anything like it in my life. I just have a hard time believing that a drug overdose caused those wounds."

Cal began flipping through the pictures and video he took on his iPhone. He showed Kelly the most graphic one causing her to almost lose control of the car. Kelly gasped in horror before Cal continued.

"I'm sure someone can tell us what happened to these boys. But we don't have a lot of time. Once their bodies are cremated, we'll never have a chance to document anything. Other than these pictures, any investigation would stop with Kevin's word."

"Cremated?"

"Yep. I saw a sheet in the lab that said all three bodies were slated for cremation on Friday."

"OK, now we know how much time we have to get to the bottom of this."

Kelly pulled onto the highway in the direction of *The Register*'s office.

CHAPTER 16

WHEN CAL TURNED ON his phone in the exam room he noticed one missed call from Guy. After he showed Kelly the pictures, he saw a notification for three new voicemails awaiting him, presumably all from Guy. He flipped through the pictures again.

Both were silent for the first few minutes of the ride, mulling over the day's events and trying to make sense of them.

Questions mounted in Cal's head. *Was a serial killer on the loose? Was there something in the water? Could there be a real Statenville Sasquatch? Did those boys simply kill themselves in a bizarre way? Or did they belong to a cult and take their devotion too far one day?* He barely had time to consider a theory or an idea before he had to draw a more definitive conclusion and move on to the next one.

It gave Cal a new appreciation for those days when his biggest assignment was taking grip-and-grin photos at the latest service club meeting. Covering these three bizarre deaths was like living in an episode of the *X-Files*. He glanced at Kelly... she had begun to remind him of Scully. Then he snapped back to reality. *Maybe they were murders. Maybe they were accidents. Maybe no one would ever know.* Cal was determined to uncover the truth.

Guy's mug shot replaced the photo of Cody Murray's body on the screen of Cal's iPhone. The phone kept buzzing, but Cal remained frozen.

"Kelly, it's the boss. What do you suggest that I tell him?" Cal asked.

"Tell him the truth."

"Are you nuts? Have you seen what kind of mood he's in today? We'll be not-so-suspicious deaths four and five if we do that."

"And you think lying now only to get found out later is better? You know he'll find out Cal… sooner or later. The man has eyes and ears everywhere."

"You're probably right."

"Look, just don't tell him about your photos. Don't tell anyone, OK? It's for your own good. Just think of those photos as your insurance.

The phone quit buzzing. Their conversation prevented Cal from answering until he knew they were on the same page about their story.

He dialed Guy's number.

"Where have you been?! I told you to come straight back to the office. That was over an hour ago!"

"Sorry, boss. We had to pay a little visit to the coroner."

"The coroner? Who do you guys think you are? Starsky and Hutch? It's not your job to investigate a murder — it's just your job to report it."

"I understand, boss. But almost no one has been giving us straight answers today."

"That's because you're acting like a gumshoe cop instead of a journalist! Did you ever think about that, boy wonder?"

Kelly stomped on the gas pedal.

Cal knew what she was doing. He mouthed a "thank you" to her while continuing to cringe from the verbal tirade Guy was on. Guy was never this cruel in person and Cal was eager to get back in order to stop this nonsense.

***

Trailing about one hundred yards behind Kelly's car was the F-250. The driver carefully calculated where he would make his move.

But there wasn't a chance just yet. Kelly was driving through a main road that led back to downtown. All the local businesses on either side of the road made it very difficult to fulfill his mission.

He eased off the gas. He knew where they were going. Tonight would give him a better chance. He would finish his assignment then.

CHAPTER 17

WHEN CAL AND KELLY returned to *The Register*, the newsroom was still full of faithful staff, preparing as much of the paper as they could for that week's edition slated to go to press Tuesday night. Cal's deadline was more than 24 hours away, but he still needed to do some of his other mundane duties before he called it a day.

Cal could sense Guy's growing angst as the day progressed, but by 5:30 in the evening, angst had given way to dirty office politics and the abuse of power. By the way Guy was acting on the phone, Cal guessed Guy hadn't even stepped outside *The Register's* office all day for anything other than a smoke break. But Cal never would've guessed what came out of Guys' mouth next.

"I hope you've got something for a reaction piece cause this is all you're writing, understand?" Guy bellowed from behind his desk.

A reaction piece? In the journalism world, a reaction piece is slightly above a man-on-the-street poll. It's a story that just about any numbskull can write without screwing up. You talk to people about a certain topic or issue or event. You quote them. They are the story. The "reporter" more or less transcribed an interview. Even a high school intern could do it.

With that re-assignment, Cal's spirit was crushed. Pulitzer award-winning story? Gone. Strong article for the clip file? Doubtful. Cal's Monday started with so much promise, but hope for a positive conclusion was fleeting faster than William Hung's 15 minutes of fame.

He almost took it without a word. Almost.

"Seriously, Guy? A *reaction piece?* I've been tracking down this story all day long and there's more to it than three teens overdosing on drugs—that much I'm sure of."

"In case you've forgotten, this is Mayberry, not New York City. Sensationalizing the unfortunate death of these kids is not something that people here want to read. So, unless you've got something other than the off-the-record whispers and innuendos you mentioned earlier, I'm not interested."

"But, boss—"

"Are you that slow, Cal? We're not doing a triple deck murder story headline, especially when there wasn't a murder. Now go get me a cutline for that board of education meeting you covered last Thursday and get out of here."

The problem with protesting one of Guy's decisions in *The Register's* tiny office was that everyone heard him dressing you down. Cal took Guy's rare tirades better than most, a sure sign that he might make it at a large daily metro. But today wasn't one of those days. Cal left Guy's office red-faced, thoroughly eviscerated professionally.

Cal began wondering what happened to Guy. *Was that serious newspaper editor once known as Guy Thompson really left for dead in Utah? As a newspaper man, there wasn't one ounce of curious intrigue into the previous 24 hours' strange happenings?* Cal had more questions than answers at this point, but he found it odd that his editor was more concerned with his whereabouts than his findings.

Cal sat down at his desk and obliged Guy. He pounded out the cutline and filed it. He spent the next hour working on some rewrites Terry requested for Wednesday's edition. Most days, Cal didn't mind Terry's editing, but Cal was in a mood, thanks to Guy. *Must he make my report on the Rotary Club meeting sound like an act from a Shakespeare play?*

"Thy edits are complete, my Lordship," Cal said to Terry in a mocking tone.

Terry furrowed his brow and squinted. The context of Cal's medieval language was obviously lost on him. He grunted a "thanks" and looked back at his computer screen. But such interactions weren't unusual for *The Register* newsroom, known for attracting more oddball personalities than a traveling circus.

By 6:30, Cal began gathering his notes and stuffing them into his briefcase, willing to follow up with some phone calls from home. He hoped to bring something substantial into the office to change Guy's mind.

He glanced back at Kelly, who was preparing to leave as well. At least the day wasn't a total waste. Spending it with her and all her spunk made everything else palatable.

Cal broke the silence.

"Ready to do it again tomorrow?"

"Yeah. Today was fun, wasn't it? But I don't see how tomorrow could be any more interesting than today."

Cal then noticed Kelly sliding a small piece of paper with a note scrawled on it.

"Call my cell when you get in your car."

Cal slid the note off her desk and into his pocket. *Maybe I won't be making some extra phone calls tonight.*

The two walked in silence through the alley and into the employee parking lot located behind *The Register*'s office building.

Cal threw his briefcase on the passenger side floorboard and pulled out his cell phone. He dialed Kelly's number.

"OK, so we know some crazy stuff is going on and Guy is acting weird, right?" Kelly began.

"Yeah, so?"

"Well, get this. I went to the break room to buy a soda and I saw the door to the outside was cracked. I went over to shut it when I heard Guy talking on his cell phone in a hushed voice."

"What did he say?"

"I didn't catch the whole thing, but I did hear him say, 'Don't worry. I've got those two under control.'"

"You think he was talking about us?"

"Who else would he be talking about?"

"It could be two of *anything* that he has under control."

"Yeah, but saying that *and* talking in a hushed tone so no one could hear him? Plus he was on his personal cell phone standing outside. It was not typical behavior for Guy."

"That might explain why he's been acting the way he has toward us. He certainly seems hell-bent on helping us avoid proper treatment of this story."

"Well, something is up and I don't like it. I'm starting to get a strange feeling about this whole thing, like we're rattling the closet door to some big skeletons. And I feel uneasy about what might happen to us."

"Seriously? Are you scared, Kelly?"

"A little, maybe. I sure would like to have a drink and throw darts at The Mill about right now. You up for joining me?"

Whoa! Is Kelly asking me out on a date? It sure sounds like it.

"Uh, sure. I want to run home and change first and then I'll meet you there in say, 30 minutes?"

"Sounds like a date."

Sounds like a date, indeed! Cal thought.

Cal and Kelly headed home in opposite directions to prepare for a rare post-work rendezvous. That is if Cal meeting Kelly once at the gas station McDonald's near the I-84 exit one night counted as a rendezvous. Otherwise, it was a first.

The F-250 followed Cal.

CHAPTER 18

AS DUSK BEGAN TO settle on the Idaho farm country, Cal turned on his headlights. He was lost in thought over the day's events and the new possibilities for the night. Then he remembered something he had hoped to extract from his busy brain before the evening was over.

Earlier in the afternoon, Cal had received a call from Josh. But with all that was going on, Cal didn't really have time to hear about how Josh's fantasy league baseball team was crushing his. Josh seemed to win their league almost every year, while Cal's team was mathematically eliminated by mid-June. He called his team "Cal's Cubs."

Josh's message oddly enough wasn't a gloating message regarding fantasy sports, but instead contained details regarding his flight information on Friday. Cal saved the message. He didn't feel like testing his multi-tasking skills: typing on his iPhone while driving.

He put the phone down and began to mentally catalog the scant information he had gathered throughout the day. He entered a winding mile stretch of road about two miles from his apartment. That's when he felt the first collision.

Bam!

Cal's car lurched forward. So did Cal.

"What the—"

Cal turned around again to see a truck's headlights roaring toward the back of his car. The truck slammed his car again and he lurched forward, bracing for the next hit.

Bam!

Chrome bumper met flimsy metal. This time Cal's car suffered a bigger blow. His Civic began spinning across the road. Cal was helpless. The steering wheel. The brakes. Nothing was his friend at the moment.

The car spun around five times before slowing down and straightening out—just in time to go careening down a shallow embankment and into a patch of woods by the Snake River.

Rock. Tree. Boulder. Tree. Shallow stream. Tree. Rock. Rock. Tree. Bushes.

Cal's car was playing chicken with the woods—and winning. No amount of strength exerted on the steering wheel would have made a difference at this point anyway. The wheels bounced the car as it gained speed.

Instead of wondering why someone would do this to him, Cal spent most of his time worrying about when his car might come to a stop. And his condition – and the car's – once it did.

Then he didn't have to wonder.

Thud!

Cal's car came to a complete stop. One seemingly unstoppable object met an unforgiving one. Cal's car was on the losing end.

Steam hissed from the front of his Civic. Mangled metal took the place of a functioning engine. Wedged between two pine trees, the car was stuck. The headlights served as obscure beacons in the dense woods.

Cal's head rested motionless on the airbag. The rest of his body didn't move either.

CHAPTER 19

NATHAN GOLD SHIFTED IN his leather reading chair. The dark oak walls with a custom-built bookcase encircled his study. They contained an extensive collection of rare books and literary masterpieces, all well worn. It was clear Gold was more interested in creating a suitable home for literature than he was for demonstrating opulence in his Tudor-style mansion. Extravagant pleasures could be found elsewhere in the house.

But tonight he wasn't thinking about his books—he was thinking about *his* town. Like the safe haven he constructed for each shelved piece of art in his library, Statenville had been effectively cocooned through careful planning. And Gold enjoyed it. Just like he enjoyed reading John Milton's *Paradise Lost*. But tonight his thoughts were distant, his gaze vacant.

His own paradise was teetering on vanishing at the hands of a pesky reporter bent on pulling back Oz's curtain. Only he didn't know he was in Oz. Gold knew that Cal didn't see Statenville as a final resting place for his career. Outsiders working at *The Register* rarely did. Statenville was a blinking yellow light along a two-lane road to somewhere else. It was a cup of coffee.

But as the day's events unfolded, Gold grew leery of a foreigner mucking about in a family matter. Gold's son had died—and he was struggling to suppress the grief he felt. He had to. There was more at stake than the personal embarrassment of his son overdosing on drugs and the paper etching it into town lore on microfilm. *Statenville* was at stake.

Cal had no idea what he was doing, but it made no difference to Gold. As the mayor of Statenville, Gold prided himself on his moral and ethical conduct. But it was easy to justify a temporary restraining order on such morals and ethics when your way of life is being threatened. Gold knew it would be a tough decision to make, but it was for the good of the whole. At least that's what he told himself.

He took a long pull on his glass of scotch. He pondered his next move.

His phone rang and a voice on the other end gave him the news: "Cal's gone."

"What? Where is he? What about the girl?"

"His car veered off the road and wrecked near the river, but he was nowhere to be found. The girl's still waiting for him at The Mill, but she's lost without him. She still thinks that one day she might run *The Register*. She'll not want to jeopardize that pipe dream, so don't worry about her."

"Well, find him. And when you do, make sure he doesn't go anywhere. Who knows where is he, now that we can't track him."

Gold hung up his phone. Grieving in peace would have to wait.

CHAPTER 20

KELLY FINISHED TROUNCING HER third darts opponent
at The Mill. Beating drunk farm boys who thought they had a
chance with her amused Kelly. She even dated a few of the regulars
in high school, back when she thought being a farmer's wife was
her destiny. She wasn't completely opposed to the idea, but working for the student paper at Arizona State gave her a taste of real
journalism—one that couldn't be quenched by whipping up
lunchtime feasts, changing little ones' diapers, and serving on the
Statenville PTA. Of course, working for *The Register* wouldn't
guarantee her more than a skimpy serving of real journalism either,
but she thought it could be palatable, especially if she were in
charge.

Kelly picked up her phone to call Cal. *Where is he? Surely he
would have called me if something came up.*

Kelly accessed his number on the screen—and hesitated. She had
already called him three times and left messages. But a *fourth?* That
might be pushing it. He was only about an hour late. No need to
seem desperate, especially for a guy she wasn't completely sure she
liked romantically. Although the exciting day's events had changed
that. Adventure proved to be a powerful elixir for her cold feet.

A basket of fries, two more dart annihilations and 45 minutes
later, Kelly decided Cal wasn't coming.

A thought crept into her mind. It was not worth mulling over, but Kelly couldn't make it go away.

What if someone doesn't want Cal to write that story? What if someone did something to him?

Her efforts to dismiss such depressing thoughts only served to stir her angst. She grabbed her purse and coat. She needed to put these hair-brained ideas to rest.

She left the bar without a word or a glance over her shoulder. This wasn't about a sudden crush on Cal. This was about her co-worker who was being threatened for doing his job.

Paranoia settled over her like a thick fog. She began scanning the parking lot for any suspicious activity or likely suspects in dark cars awaiting a certain patron. She spotted one man who looked out of place in Statenville. A new black Chevy Blazer in Statenville? He might as well have painted the car fire engine red. This was Ford country, save a few granola types who preferred Subarus. But she quickly dismissed him as her guy. He was looking down at his phone and talking to someone as he waved his free hand around. In the 10 seconds she watched him as she walked to her car, he never once looked up.

Nevertheless, Kelly quickened her pace. She fumbled for her keys as she walked, hoping to avert a prolonged mining expedition in her purse. The less vulnerable she was before gaining entrance to her car, the better.

Success.

She unlocked the door with the click of a button on her fob and slid behind the wheel. She locked the doors and turned the ignition. Before turning on her headlights, Kelly scanned one final time around the parking lot and concluded she was safe. She pulled onto the road and headed for Cal's house, using the same route he would have taken to get there.

Kelly eased down the road, searching the roadside for any sign of Cal or his Civic.

Why didn't he call me?

One jalopy and a flat tire sidelined two vehicles along the route Kelly took. No sign of Cal.

She drove another five minutes before entering a winding stretch of road near Cal's apartment.

That's where she saw the flashing lights. Red and blue squad car lights flickered in the cool August air. A squad car was on the shoulder of the road ahead. It flanked an A-1 Towing Service truck, which made its presence known with a pair of flashing yellow lights.

Kelly didn't want to presume she knew Cal was the reason for the roadside gathering, but she couldn't stop her mind from racing through all the doomsday scenarios. *Maybe Cal crashed. Maybe someone killed him. Maybe there's nothing to see.*

She sped up and pulled behind the sheriff's deputy car. It belonged to Dawkins. She closed her eyes and moaned. *Not Dawkins! Not now!*

Dawkins was talking with the tow truck driver when her headlights signaled her arrival. He turned toward her and shielded his eyes from her car lights. The deputy approached Kelly's car as she moved to meet him half way.

"What's going on here?" she asked nervously.

"Well, I thought maybe *you* could tell *us* something."

"What do you mean?"

"Mercer was off duty tonight but he called me about a car that he noticed had spun off the road. He said it was all smashed up against a tree, so I came down here to check it out. It's Cal's."

Kelly tried to ignore her emotions and get into her reporter mindset. There were questions. Lots of them. And she needed answers now.

"Have you been down there?" Kelly asked, motioning toward the ravine below.

"Yeah."

"And?"

"And what?"

"Is Cal hurt? Injured? Where is he?"

"When I went down there, I didn't see anyone."

"What do you mean, you didn't see anyone?"

"I mean, it's obviously a one-car accident. It looks like the impact with a tree crumpled the hood up pretty good. But nobody saw it happen. At least, there were no citizen reports of a driver veering off the road and into the woods."

"So, he's just gone?"

"Yep, as far as I can tell."

"Do you think he's still alive?"

Dawkins paused as if he was unsure of what to say, unsure of telling her the truth.

"There's no way to know for sure. It's hard to imagine him just getting out of that car, wrecked the way that it is, and just walking around. But we'll keep looking."

"Well, please call me on my cell if you find him."

Kelly handed him her business card and began walking back to her car. She thought she might be able to make Dawkins crack. A little flirtatious behavior never hurt with law enforcement types when it came to getting what she wanted. But she left feeling like she didn't get what she needed out of him.

Then there was a more pressing matter: Cal could be dead.

CHAPTER 21

DAWKINS SMILED AS HE walked back to his car. The more lies he told, the easier it got—even if he didn't like it. Now he had lied twice in one day to Kelly. He wouldn't let her beauty distract him from following his new orders. A night worrying about Cal would make her putty in the boss's hands. And that's what they needed at the moment since Cal was now missing and up to who knows what. Kelly wouldn't think straight. Three boys would be buried on Saturday. Statenville would move on by the time she thought about revisiting the suspicious information she and Cal were gathering.

But there was a problem. A big problem.

For all of Dawkins' lies, he didn't know the full truth himself. The part he really cared about was Cal's whereabouts. Cal was missing. How his car eluded the onslaught of obstacles down the hill until making a soft enough landing in the trees for him to walk away was nothing short of a miracle. But who sent him careening off the road was a bigger mystery at the moment.

By the time Dawkins arrived on the scene and found Cal's car in the woods, Cal was gone. Did he stumble off into the woods alone? Did someone help him? What happened? Suddenly the protector of one mystery found himself wondering about another.

Just where was Cal Murphy?

CHAPTER 22

WHEN CAL CAME TO, the massive migraine throbbing in his head was quickly forgotten. He was gagged and tied to a chair with duct tape. The solitary light bulb hanging inches from his face was blinding. The smell of manure emanated from the dirt floor. *Where am I? Why am I tied to a chair?*

Cal remembered getting hit from behind and bounding down a hill where he came to a sudden but safe stop. The airbags deployed but he was just fine. He was stepping out of the car when two men injected him with a needle. That was the last thing he remembered. Cal was just now realizing that the needle contained a sedative—and he had no idea how long he had been out. An hour? A day? A week? There was no way of knowing for sure.

Just as Cal was ordering his thoughts, a man wearing a ski mask squatted in front of Cal and began questioning him in a smooth, calm voice.

"Are you Cal Murphy?"

"What is this?"

"Answer my question, please."

"Yeah, I'm Cal Murphy. What are you doing to me?!"

"Please, Cal. Just remain calm, answer my questions and you'll be out of here in no time."

"Whatever, man. This is kidnapping. You're going to jail."

"Don't make empty threats and hollow promises, boy. You and I both know that won't happen. The men guiding this venture will never let that happen. So, you better just get comfortable with the idea that cooperation is in your best interest."

Cal gritted his teeth. In a moment like this, restraint escaped him. He usually wanted justice—and he wanted it yesterday. But for all the mystery surrounding the deaths of the three teens in Statenville, he wanted to get some answers before getting offed. This story was not going find its way into print or online anytime soon anyway, so no need to push where pushing only led to trouble.

He decided to play along.

"OK, what do you want me to do?"

"Back off! If you keep digging into the death of these three teens, you're going to write about some things that are going to anger plenty of people. Your safety will be at stake. Your life may be as well."

"I can't back off now, especially when I'm obviously rattling the cage of somebody somewhere."

"You will have a lifetime to spin the tale of the three teens' deaths. Now is not the time to rip open the heart of a grieving community. Wait a few months to disclose what you know and you'll be duly rewarded."

"A few *months*?! You mean to tell me that you kidnapped me and risked many other things just to tell me *that*?"

"My motivation is none of your concern. Your concern is following orders. Got it?"

"Yeah. I got it."

"Good. I'm glad we could have this conversation."

With that, the masked man punctured Cal's neck with a needle, injecting another dose of the fast-acting sedative. Cal's vision dimmed, then his head drooped.

CHAPTER 23

GOLD DIDN'T LIKE LOOSE ends, but by midnight he had one.

His goon's attempt at silencing Cal took an unfortunate turn when Cal not only survived the bump off the road, but he vanished as well. This was not the kind of news Gold ever enjoyed hearing, particularly after he had gone to bed thinking his kingdom was safe again.

"Have you found him yet?" Gold barked into his phone.

"No, sir. Don't worry though. We'll take care of it."

"You said that last time."

"Don't worry. We'll keep him out of the way."

"Good. I don't want to lose any more sleep over this, you hear?"

"Yes, sir."

Gold loved ordering the Sheriff around like that. It was one of the perks of controlling a town and its dark secrets. Hunter Jones owed Gold everything, so when Gold said, "Jump," Jones always asked, "Where to?" It was that easy for Gold.

* * *

Jones loathed the way Gold treated him. After all, wasn't *he* the sheriff? Instead, it seemed like Gold thought he was the one with a badge—and never had to get his hands dirty. Tonight, Jones was about to get grime beneath his fingernails for a good cause.

He dialed Dawkins' number.

"Yeah, boss."

"You found Cal yet?"

"Nope. We're still looking."

"Well, when you do, charge him with driving under the influence."

"We can't do that."

"Dawkins, have you lost your mind? You know we can do anything we want in this town. I got a call from dispatch that a car matching Cal's was weaving all over the road. Do you need any more than that?"

"No, sir. I think I can make that work. We'll find him."

CHAPTER 24

CAL'S IPHONE WAS PROGRAMMED to awaken him at 8 a.m. every Tuesday. It was his deadline day. *The Register* went to press every Tuesday at 8:30 p.m. rarely without exception.

The last time the presses were held was two years ago when Paul Hackett brought his pick axe to a board of education meeting and threatened one of the board members. When the appropriately named Hackett waved his axe within inches of the board member's face, Kelly snapped a photo. With barely six months of experience under her belt, she managed to convince Guy to hold the presses. It turned out to be good journalistic instincts by everyone as the photo won best news action shot for an Idaho weekly.

Cal's iPhone chimed an airy melody. He didn't move much.

Cal was groggy. The wild events of the night before left him wondering if it wasn't all a bad dream. There he was in his bed with his clothes on. *What happened?*

Cal stumbled into the shower, hoping hot water might rouse him to his senses. Slowly, it began to come back to him. He was meeting Kelly. Then someone hit him from behind on purpose. He slid off the road. He survived the spill down the hill. Someone drugged him, warned him to back off, and put him to sleep in his apartment.

Without a second thought, Cal dashed to the window to look

for his car. It wasn't there.

Cal returned to the shower, trying to squeeze out more details from his beleaguered memory. Who took him? Where did they take him? And why? Why warn him to wait before releasing the story?

None of it made sense. Cal's initial hypothesis was that someone ran him off the road because he got too close to the truth about the teens' deaths. Or at least they thought he was getting close. Cal felt like he was no closer at that moment than he was 24 hours before when he was taking a shower just after hearing the news from Guy.

Not that it really mattered anyway. Guy had assigned him a benign reaction piece—and Cal doubted Tuesday before deadline was enough time to sway Guy's opinion to allow him to write the real story. Especially when Cal had nothing but the memory of those boys' mutilated bodies in his mind.

Cal finished his shower, toweled off and dialed Kelly's number.

"Cal? Is that you?!" Kelly asked without the slightest thought of a greeting.

"Yeah, Kelly. I'm OK. Sorry about last night."

"Sorry about last night? Are you kidding me? I'm just glad you're alive. I thought you were dead after I heard your car went off the road and they couldn't find you."

Cal cringed. He remembered his car had been wrecked. While it was the least of his worries, he hated the hassle of being without a car and having to get it repaired.

"Yeah, I'm gonna need a ride this morning."

"Don't worry. I'll come get you. Be there in 15 minutes."

Cal finished getting dressed and mulled over the previous night's events. He wasn't close to having all the facts or even close enough to the truth to form a fledgling theory to float to Guy. But he knew that whatever information he had led to something more. Maybe it was sinister. Maybe it was corruption. Maybe it was a cover up. Maybe …

Conspiracy theorists irked Cal, but he couldn't help himself. *Something* was going on, and *somebody* didn't want him to find out what. Unraveling the mystery was as simple as that—find out who the somebody is and learn what the something is. But there was nothing simple about it.

Cal's mind whirled with ideas. Did he hear helicopters overhead? Did a special ops guy rush him from the river where he had been lying in wait? Cal's imagination was beginning to drift when the beeping of Kelly's car horn broke his trance.

He grabbed his iPhone and his keys and glanced back at his room before he headed out. Then he noticed a note lying unopened on his dresser. It was addressed to him: "Mr. Cal Murphy."

Ding, Dong! Cal realized that Kelly was anxious to see him.

Cal stuffed the envelope into his pocket and headed for the front door.

CHAPTER 25

ON THE DOORSTEP OF Cal's apartment, Kelly greeted Cal with a hug that pushed the limits of simple friendship. It was extra tight with a final squeeze before letting go. In his oblivious state, Cal had no idea how worried Kelly was over his short disappearance. What seemed like a bad dream to Cal was a living nightmare for Kelly.

"I'm so glad you're OK," Kelly said as she turned toward her car.

"Me, too."

Kelly fired up her Charger and began seeking details.

"So, what happened last night? How did your car end up in a ditch? How did you get home? Did this have anything to do with the case?"

"All I remember is that a big truck bumped me from behind a couple of times and forced me off the road. When the car came to a stop, the air bags deployed. I remember trying to get out to inspect the damage and then I blacked out. When I came to, I was bound to a chair with duct tape and some guys in ski masks told me to stop sticking my nose where it didn't belong. Then, the next thing I know, I'm waking up in my own bed."

"That's it? Nothing else?"

Cal fidgeted with the envelope in his pocket. After a moment's hesitation, he pulled it out. After the events of the previous 24 hours, he trusted no one—except Kelly.

"The only clue I might have is this letter I found on my dresser this morning."

Cal opened the letter and began reading it to himself. However, it wasn't fast enough for Kelly's inquiring mind.

"What does it say?"

"This is creepy."

"What does it say?"

"OK, here it goes," Cal said as he began reading the letter aloud.

Mr. Murphy,

We apologize for last night's rude introduction, albeit one without names and faces. I'm sure you have many questions, but now is not the time to give you all the answers. We view you as an important ally, but strongly urge you to keep the events of last night to yourself and create a good cover story. We have plenty of information to give you, but the timing is not right yet. There are some things happening in your community that would put you at risk if you knew them. The best thing for you to do is to keep quiet and do your job without asking any questions.

When the time is right, we will present you with information that will surely land you in the national spotlight for your reporting skills. If you should choose to ignore our strong suggestion, we do have other ways of persuasion. And I can assure you that you're best off not experiencing them.

We trust you will show this to no one or tell anyone about this letter or the truth about last night's events, including Kelly or Guy. Until we meet again …

"This is disturbing, to say the least."

"You're telling me. How do they know *my* name?"

"I don't know, but I've already done two things I wasn't supposed to do—tell you what really happened and read you this letter."

"Don't worry, Cal. Your secret is safe with me—unless something horrible happens."

"Oh, Kelly. There's no need to be so dramatic. Nothing is going to happen to me."

"Are you crazy? You could've been killed last night by some se-cret government group or something – or died when your car smashed into a tree."

Cal stopped.

"Who told you I smashed into a tree?"

"Dawkins did last night. I went looking for you and I pulled off the road next to his squad car and a tow truck. Then he showed me where your car landed."

"My car? It was smashed up?"

"Well, I couldn't see it because it was so dark, but he told me it was."

"I don't remember much, but I do remember coming to a stop between a pair of trees. My car wasn't smashed as I recall. It just came to a sudden stop in between two trees and that forced out my airbag. But it wasn't *that* bad. I wonder why Dawkins would lie to you like that."

Silence hung in the air as both tried to form a hypothesis. Cal concluded there was only one logical explanation: Dawkins was in on some sheriff's office plot to stop him from digging into the deaths of Statenville's three football heroes.

After a few minutes of breaking down their theories, Cal accessed all his steely resolve and boldly staked his pursuit of the truth.

"If someone is trying to kill me and make it look like an accident or cover it up—or if somebody just wants to keep me quiet for a while—then I must be close to some pretty big secrets that pow-erful people don't want uncovered. But it seems like there's more than one secret. This town doesn't want me to know something—and neither do some mysterious kidnappers. But this is great – I went into journalism to expose coverups like this!"

Cal glanced at Kelly and caught her smiling, as if she were proud of something.

"I don't care what Guy says, I'm going to keep digging on this case. But let's keep it on the down low, OK? Writing my reaction piece will be my cover for seeing what else I can find out. I have a good feeling about today."

Kelly rounded the corner at the traffic light just one block from *The Register*'s office. Two deputy cars were parked outside the entrance with their lights flashing. Dawkins and Sheriff Jones were leaning against their cars and staring down the street in Kelly's direction. Once they saw Kelly's car, they opened their doors and began talking on their radios.

"I wonder what this is all about," Kelly said, as she pulled off the main street to park in the back lot.

"I don't know, but that good feeling is gone."

Cal had set one foot on the gravel parking lot before Dawkins and Sheriff Jones greeted him with handcuffs.

"Cal Murphy, you're under arrest."

CHAPTER 26

THE STATENVILLE JAIL WAS little more than a holding cell. Sheriff Jones wasn't interested in wasting the taxpayers' hard-earned money by making his jail a comfortable place for the community's riff raff. One concrete block wall framed by three sets of iron walls in a 10-foot by 10-foot space formed the prison. Water dripped from the ceiling and formed a stain in the corner of the dark cell. There wasn't even a bed. A stainless steel toilet provided the cell's lone décor.

Drifters and drunks usually found themselves in these cramped quarters for little more than 24 hours. Real criminals were transferred to Boise. It had been three years since Statenville had a serious crime, when Bill Peterson went on a drunken rampage and stuck his wife with a pitchfork after he found out she had been cheating on him. Since then, no real threat to Statenville's peaceful way of life had sat behind these lonely bars.

Until now.

The trumped up charges were possession of an open container and driving under the influence. Cal knew the charges would never stick in a real court of law. He didn't drink very often and certainly wasn't driving around the previous night with any alcohol in his car, opened or otherwise. But this was Statenville. He was in trouble and recognized his arrest as an over-the-top bullying tactic by someone. If there was a proper time to take a drink, now seemed appropriate.

Dawkins booked Cal and took a mug shot, hurling mocking insults at the reporter throughout the process. Cal had no idea who he could hire as a lawyer or where he would begin to look for one. Statenville's limited attorneys were out of the question.

Cal thought he was doing Statenville a favor by finding out if some malicious-minded person was behind the three suspicious deaths of these young men. But as Sheriff Jones shoved him into the cell with one other occupant, Cal figured the secret he was close to unearthing was far more threatening to some powerful people than he realized.

Cal slumped against the cell wall and stared mouth agape in no particular direction. For Cal, Tuesday had started off worse than Monday.

Sheriff Jones and Dawkins left the station, presumably to begin patrolling Statenville's streets for more benign criminal activity. The only person left was the lady running dispatch.

Cal's thoughts consumed him so much that he hardly noticed the other man sitting across from him in the cell. The man appeared to be in his late 40s, though life had been unkind to him. His beard challenged his hair for the most suitable location for a bird's nest on his body, while the combination of body odor and alcohol emanating from him ensured no bird—or person—would come near him. He wore a tattered jacket with a raggedy flannel shirt underneath. Both of his knees protruded through his jeans. Work boots donned his feet and looked like the most durable piece of clothing he owned. And for good reason. He looked the part of a drifter.

The man waited a few minutes before seizing the ear of his captive audience.

After a nervous glance around the office, the man crouched low and scrambled across the ground like some kind of wild animal and sat down next to Cal.

Cal recoiled. The man's stench alone almost forced Cal to look away and beg him to go away. His toothy grin made him look crazy.

"Willie," the man said as a way of introducing himself and put out his hand to Cal. "Willie Nelson."

Cal obliged the man with a handshake but remained withdrawn. Willie appeared to be a few rain clouds short of a thunderstorm.

Cal said nothing and waited for the craziness to commence.

"I know what you're thinkin'," Willie said. "You're thinkin' I'm crazy. Well, I might be; I'm a ramblin' man. But I know why you're here."

Cal agreed. He indeed thought Willie was crazy. But considering the fact that he was behind bars and had nothing else to do, he cautiously played along.

"Oh, you do? Well, Willie, why am I here?"

"You don't play by the rules."

Cal snickered, dismissing Willie's statement.

"Of course, I don't play by the rules, Willie. Otherwise, I would-n't be here, right?"

"No, that's not what I mean."

"Well then, what *do* you mean?"

"I mean, you don't play by *their* rules?"

"And whose rules would you be referring to?"

"The Golden Rules."

Cal was beginning to get annoyed with Willie's vague ramblings. "Ah, 'Do unto others as you would have them do unto you'? I try to live that out each day."

"Mr. Murphy, there are more powerful forces at work in this town than you can imagine. Everyone is really nice until you get close to their secret."

"How do you know my name?"

Willie ignored Cal's question.

"That's what happened to me. I found out their big secret and now look at me."

Cal didn't need to look Willie over just to reaffirm his first im-pression of how unattractive and crazy he looked. But he did it any way.

"*They* did this to you?"

"Yep, and they'll do it to you, too. I used to be a successful busi-nessman in this community, but I lost it all once I found out."

"Really? And what was this secret?"

"Are you listening to me, Mr. Murphy? Once you learn a secret, you can never unlearn it. And you don't want to learn this one. If you found out, you'd try to print it in that newspaper you write for—and before it ever made it to the press, they'd know that you know their secret. That's when they would turn you into someone like me. Or, if you're lucky, they'd kill you."

Cal forced a nervous laugh. Willie seemed crazier by the moment, but Cal grew uneasy with the direction of the conversation. *What if this crazy old man was telling the truth?*

* * *

Once Guy calmed down, he walked down the street to bail Cal out of jail. He met Sheriff Jones in the lobby and together they made their way to the holding cell where they entered unannounced.

"Willie, what are you telling Cal?" bellowed Sheriff Jones.

"I'm not tellin' him anything you don't already know, Sheriff," Willie said defiantly.

Sheriff Jones laughed.

"Crazy Willie, you are one of a kind."

The Sheriff dismissed Willie as the crazy man that he was. It was clear Willie's conversation with Cal was over.

"Let's go, Cal. Your boss is here to bail you out."

Cal exited the cell and looked back at Willie.

"They're watching you, man. Be careful!" Willie yelled.

The uneasy feeling in Cal's stomach grew. He wanted a do-over on today and it was only 10:30 in the morning.

CHAPTER 27

GUY WAITED UNTIL HE and Cal were outside the sheriff's office before he exploded.

"What were you thinking, driving around drunk and nearly killing yourself last night?!" Guy demanded.

"I wasn't, Guy. Someone is trying to keep me quiet because I'm learning too many details about the death of those boys."

"Oh, Cal, please. Spare me the conspiracy theories."

"It's not a theory. It's – "

"It's what, Cal? Ridiculous? True? I'm not interested in any excuses you've concocted while sitting in jail talking to crazy Willie. The bottom line is you're going to be suspended after today. I'd suspend you right now but I need your help on today's paper. Starting Wednesday, you'll have a one-day suspension without pay, got it?"

"On my day off?"

Guy said nothing. Cal quickly picked up the idea that Guy was feigning anger. Why he was doing so remained a mystery for the moment.

They walked through *The Register*'s front doors before Guy picked up his tirade.

"After today, I don't want to see your suspended self down here, do you understand?"

Every newsroom employee pretended to look busy while sneaking glances at Guy and Cal walking through the office. Even Kelly wasn't sure how to react.

Cal tried to stop at his desk, but Guy nudged him forward, obviously intending for him to continue on to Guy's office.

After Cal took a seat in front of Guy's desk, Guy slammed the door. Guy sat down and then leaned across the desk. Cal leaned in too. Guy spoke only slightly more audible than a whisper.

"Cal, if you think that anger was for show, it won't be if you don't drop your little Sherlock Holmes fantasy. I know it might be difficult as a reporter to stop looking for the truth on a story, but I'm begging you to stop for your own good."

Confusion spread over Cal's face.

"What is going on here? Don't you want me to find out what's going on?" he asked back, matching Guy's hushed tone.

"If I did, Cal, I wouldn't have assigned you a simple reaction piece. God knows Sammy couldn't ferret out the truth for a news story if his life depended on it. I'm just asking you to do this as a friend. Can you do that for me?"

"OK, Guy. I guess I can just drop it."

"I don't mean just say you're going to drop it. I mean drop it, period. No off-the-clock digging. No asking any more questions. Nothing. Got it?"

"But, Guy, you don't know what I saw when I looked at those bodies at the coroner's office. It looked like – "

"No, no, no. I don't want to hear it, Cal. I don't care if it looked like a mountain lion attack. It's not important as far as I'm concerned."

"Not important? You're the managing editor! I thought the truth was important to you no matter what the cost."

"The truth is overpriced sometimes. Just lay off it, OK?"

Cal let out a big breath and then nodded.

"OK, Guy. I'll let this go for you."

"No, don't do it for me. Do it for yourself because if you don't, you'll find out what I mean. Now, go finish that reaction piece. I need it by 1:30."

Cal left Guy's office in a huff, more out of show than frustration—but both were clearly in play. He stopped at Kelly's desk and continued talking in a hushed tone.

"We need to talk. Got any lunch plans?"

The rest of the morning, Cal worked the phones, calling a few people who knew more than one of the teens who had died. He figured if he wasn't going to get an award-winning story, he might as well polish what he did write for inclusion in his clip file.

He talked to teachers and little league coaches and employers and family members. He looked at the teens' Facebook pages. Friends posted their favorite memories of them, some without discretion. They were tagged in photos from the end-of-camp cookout at Coach Walker's house on Saturday afternoon. They all looked so happy, so full of life. No more two-a-days. But now it was gone. And apparently no one really cared why.

Cal eventually exhausted every known connection to the young men before beginning to write. And write he did. By one o'clock, Cal had finished his story and was in desperate need of lunch and a serious debriefing with Kelly.

CHAPTER 28

CAL'S HEAD SPUN TRYING to process what he knew and what he wanted to know. It felt like a two-sided puzzle of the same picture with no straight edges. *If only I could start to put a few of the pieces together ...*

Kelly volunteered to drive to lunch. She was just as engrossed in the growing mysteries surrounding the events of the past 48 hours. Three dead teens overdosing on drugs. Their bodies looking as if they had been ravaged by a wild animal. Guy acting unusual at the office. The sheriff's department giving them the runaround. The near fatal crash. A clandestine kidnapping. Cal's curious return home. Trumped up charges. Brief incarceration. The ramblings of crazy Willie.

None of it made sense. Nothing. And Cal needed to sort it out with the brightest mind he worked with – and the only person he trusted at this point: Kelly.

"Where are we headed?" Kelly asked, adjusting her sunglasses for the bright early afternoon glare.

"I make a mean chicken salad sandwich."

"OK, Cal's Kitchen it is."

"You know Ray-Ray's is always my top choice, but we need to be able to talk about this stuff in private."

"I understand."

The two sat in silence for the rest of the short drive to Cal's house. Cal knew what he really needed to do was find a good lawyer during his lunch break, but this story felt more pressing.

Once they reached Cal's apartment, they both entered and began performing utilitarian functions—Cal whipped up chicken salad, while Kelly grabbed a notebook and started to look for common threads in the recent events.

"What secret could this town hold that is so important that some people would collude to do anything to keep me from knowing it?" Cal asked as he chopped up a cooked chicken breast.

"If we could answer that one on our own, Cal, we wouldn't need this conversation."

"I know, but you've lived here your whole life. Do you remember ever hearing anything that could be considered a secret to an outsider?"

"Well, I know that Paul Bridges' farm uses a pesticide on their tomatoes that was outlawed by the feds 15 years ago."

"I fail to see how that could connect to what's been going on." Kelly tapped her pen on the blank notebook.

"You've got a point. Let me think."

"Before we try to figure out the secret, let's think about this. Do all three of the grieving families have something else in common other than boys who died by being stupid and using drugs?"

"Nothing that readily comes to mind."

"And they weren't hanging out together on Sunday, were they?"

"Nope. They all went to church at their respective ward houses on Sunday morning."

"Hmm. They're all Mormon, right?"

"So is eighty percent of this town, Cal. Just take comfort in knowing that if you do get killed here, someone will be praying for you after you're gone."

"And you won't be, Kelly?"

"What? You think I'm a Mormon?"

"Yeah. You aren't?"

"I don't like anyone telling me what to do."

"You did graduate from high school and college—two places where someone tells you where to be and what to do and when to do it. And now you have a job..."

"OK, OK. I'm not quite the rebel I make myself out to be. I don't know why I don't like religion, but it just didn't feel right to me. My family's definitely not happy about it, but they'll get over it eventually."

"Obviously, the link to faith is a moot point in this case. What else?"

Cal had finished making the chicken salad and was slathering his gourmet concoction all over toasted sandwich bread for the two of them. He handed her the sandwich. She then took a sizable bite and told him how impressed she was with his cooking prowess. Then she answered his question.

"Nothing that I can think of. Their parents all work in different places and live in different areas of town. The only thing I can think of is that they all played football together."

Cal suddenly got excited.

"That's right! They all played football together."

"Cal, I swear you'd get excited about finding a nickel in your favor on your bank statement. Of course they played football together."

"No, no, no. I mean, that's the last time they were all seen together. I should look through those photos and see if I can identify any of the other kids and ask them about what they saw or what they might know."

"OK, 'party at Coach Walker's house' is going down on the pad," said Kelly as she scratched out her first visible connection.

Despite the first breakthrough, Cal was beginning to feel hopeless.

"But who were those guys who kidnapped me?"

Kelly was getting annoyed with Cal's non-existent sleuthing skills. Neither of them were asking the right questions—and they knew it. They needed a break.

After cramming the last piece of her sandwich into her mouth, Kelly headed toward the door.

"I need some fresh air," she said.

Cal deposited all the dishes into the sink before sitting down at the table to ponder what he knew—and what blanks were left to fill in. It was almost all of them.

Just as he was considering taking the advice of the mysterious note left for him earlier that day and doing nothing, Kelly raced back through the front door and started yelling hysterically.

"There's a black van that just pulled up across the parking lot and the guy in the driver's side was wearing a ski mask!"

Cal hunched down and peered out the window. Two men dressed in all black carrying assault weapons were running across the parking lot toward his apartment building.

He grabbed Kelly's hand and began formulating a plan.

"Follow me!"

Kelly grabbed her bag but left the notepad, hoping that whoever was pursuing them would discover by the near-blank paper's admission that they knew little to nothing.

They ran out the back door and toward the small private garages behind the apartment unit. Cal fumbled for his keys as he ran and managed to jam the key into the lock on his first attempt. He slammed the door behind them.

"What are we doing?" Kelly shrieked.

Cal ignored her and finished uncovering the motorcycle in the corner.

"What is this?" Kelly asked.

"It's what's gonna save our lives. Get on."

Cal had pushed the motorcycle near the door and was now stomping on the foot crank. On the second kick, the bike roared to life. Kelly climbed on and Cal swung open the door.

The Honda 280XR dirt bike wasn't the fastest bike, but it had some much-needed zero-to-sixty acceleration. It was exactly what Cal needed right then.

Cal guessed the two men would split up, with one coming around the front and one coming around the near side of the building. He pointed the bike toward the far side of the building and opened the engine wide open.

He looked back over his shoulder to see one of the two men taking aim with an automatic assault weapon. A few stray bullets whizzed past their heads. Kelly screamed in terror. Cal suppressed his desire to join her. He banked left and rounded the building.

He then headed straight for the farthest exit in hopes of losing the men.

Cal's strategy worked brilliantly. After another 30 seconds of riding, the two men couldn't be seen. The last image Cal had of them was a mad dash to their truck, but he knew he would be long gone by then.

Cal knew a place they would never find him.

CHAPTER 29

"I THINK WE'RE IN the clear now," Cal shouted over his shoulder at Kelly.

He had only driven about 100 yards past the entrance to his apartment complex before veering onto a dirt road.

"Yeah, but for how long?"

Kelly looked like a contestant on a reality TV show after being told that she would get $100,000 if she laid in an enclosed glass case full of tarantulas. Adding to that look were wind-forced tears that had streaked mascara down her face during the getaway.

Cal still thought she looked cute.

"Just hold tight. I'm heading to a place where they won't find us."

"Where's that?"

"Devil's Canyon."

Devil's Canyon was a dirt bike enthusiast's heaven. Rolling dirt hills, devoid of any man-made objects, for miles. Four-wheeled vehicles didn't do well in Devil's Canyon. Even Land Rovers and Jeeps struggled. There were plenty of caves as well to hide in should someone spot them. At this time of day, everything was quiet. But by four o'clock, Devil's Canyon would be humming with the buzz of two-stroke engines. It was two o'clock and they needed to be gone before all the riders descended there.

In this vast expanse of space, Cal knew his dirt biking skills would serve him well. The only potential pit fall was the long chain-link fence that served as a surprisingly secure perimeter for the back property of Cloverdale Industries, nearly two miles away. But riding toward it would be pointless anyway, like running upstairs in a horror movie to escape the slow-walking villain.

Cal drove toward his favorite cave to provide some cover from the blazing sun and to hide from any curious onlookers. He helped Kelly off first before putting down his kickstand and climbing off the bike.

Kelly shook for two minutes after getting off the bike.

"Cal, we are in way over our heads," she finally muttered.

Cal said nothing and shook his head. He was scared, but equally perplexed over why someone wanted to kill him. *What did I do? What secret am I close to?*

"What are we gonna do?"

Kelly needed answers. She needed assurance. Tough and tender. She was both, but her tough side was curled up in a corner wishing that their near-death experience was nothing more than a bad dream. It wasn't.

Cal collected his thoughts and finally began to give Kelly something else she needed: a plan.

"I think we should lay low for an hour or so and then try to get back to town. Maybe we can call Guy."

"Are you crazy? He'll fire you if he finds out what happened. He'll jump to the conclusion that you were doing what he told you not to do and then tell you to take a hike. A storm cloud of suspicion was already forming over you before this happened."

"You're right. The problem is there's only one person in this town that I trust at the moment—and that's you."

Cal pulled his iPhone out of his pocket. He had no cell tower coverage anyway, so the idea was moot.

"If we're gone long, there's going to be an all-out hunt for us. You remember what happened when the Atkins' girl wandered off her family's ranch? There was a team of more than 100 people combing the hills for her. They're going to come looking for us like that."

"That might not be such a bad idea."

"Or it could be a terrible thing. More than one person in this town seems intent on keeping the truth buried."

"OK, OK. Let's just think about what plan of action makes the most sense."

The next 10 minutes were an exercise in futility. The beginning of an idea would be proffered only to be instantly shot down. Just like their investigation, they were going nowhere.

Then Cal stopped.

"Do you hear that?" he said, squinting south toward the direction of the main road leading into Devil's Canyon.

"Yeah, it sounds like some dirt bikes are headed this way."

Kelly joined him in peering out across the dirt hills, searching for the first glimpse of another rider. The westerly prevailing winds thrashed the desert dirt floor and carried the faint sounds of a motorcycle.

In a matter of seconds, it was clear the bike was headed toward their location. Cal wasn't sure if he wanted to solicit the help of a stranger or not. He wanted to see his potential aid first before making a decision.

The buzzing engine got louder and louder. Cal could tell there was more than one bike. Neither he nor Kelly moved, almost holding their breaths. They were both hoping for someone who could help.

Finally, about 400 yards away, a bike appeared. But it wasn't what Cal and Kelly were hoping for.

The first of the two armed gunmen was barreling toward them.

CHAPTER 30

"GET ON NOW!" CAL screamed, straddling the bike and stomping on the kick start.

Kelly almost beat him to the bike. Cal revved the engine and released the clutch, hoping to minimize the distance their assailants could gain before coming up with a good escape plan.

Cal looked over his shoulder. They were 300 yards away and closing. Cal's bike still hadn't reached top speed, and his pursuers obviously had several hundred yards back. Kelly pulled close. Cal headed west.

With nothing for several miles in either direction, Cal's goal was to make it to the edge of the wooded area with enough vegetation to hide out. It wasn't a fail-proof plan, but it was a plan.

Now they were getting dangerously close. Only two more miles to go. Cal wondered if he could make it to the woods with enough time to hide?

Over the next mile and a half, Cal gauged that the pursuers hadn't gained much ground. Cal then began shouting his idea over his shoulder to Kelly.

With about 50 yards to go, Cal noticed that the back perimeter fence of Cloverdale Industries adjacent to the wooded area had a sizeable hole beneath it. The only problem was an eight-foot-deep creek bed that was about six feet across and presented a moderate challenge to reaching the other side. They could try to lay low in the brush and hope the gunmen didn't find them. Or they could try to jump across the creek.

As Cal quickly surveyed the approaching woods, leaping across the creek seemed like their best option. He instructed Kelly on what to do.

The gunmen were still pursuing them at full speed.

Cal drove 30 yards into the woods, sufficient to obstruct the closing gunmen's view with thick brush. He and Kelly jumped off the bike. Cal revved the engine and shoved it in the opposite direction, hoping to gain a few more valuable seconds for their getaway.

They ran to the edge of the bank. Kelly gasped.

"I don't think I can do this, Cal."

"Don't think about how far across it is right now. Just jump. Come on."

Cal backed up a few steps for a running start and leaped, landing on the other side of the bank with relative ease.

The engines buzzed louder with each passing second.

"Come on, Kelly. Trust me. You can do this."

Kelly tossed her backpack over to Cal and backed up a few steps. Cal looked east through the woods and saw the gunmen within about five seconds of reaching the woods. Kelly took off running.

As Kelly reached the lip of the bank, she stepped too far out on the edge. The loose dirt gave way and Kelly went feet first into the creek.

The small splash she made in the ankle-deep water was inaudible to the gunmen, who were still on their motorcycles and combing the area where Cal had shoved the bike. They never heard her or her colorful language.

"Come on, Kelly. Give me your hand," Cal said barely above a whisper.

Kelly sloshed across the creek toward Cal's outstretched hand. Cal could only monitor her progress with his peripheral vision as he never lost sight of the gunmen. He had to save Kelly but he also had to tell this story, one no one would ever hear about it if they were murdered in the woods. If Statenville treated their deaths like they had the deaths of the three teenagers, nobody would ever care about how these two reporters died—nor would anyone ever discover the truth. There would be no TV news special to answer the unexplainable disappearance of two up-and-coming journalists.

Cal heard the men yelling at one another. Their bikes idled as they fanned out and searched on foot. They still failed to look in the direction of the creek.

"Hurry up, Kelly!"

For Cal, each second lasted as long as a day of typing obituaries.

Kelly finally made it to Cal. She grabbed his hand tightly as he hoisted her slender frame up an additional three feet and onto the other bank.

"Go, go, go," Cal said, shoving Kelly underneath the fence.

Cal continued to keep watch as she crawled onto Cloverdale Industries property. Once she was through, Cal began slithering backward under the fence. The gunmen then turned off their bikes but continued to search in other directions.

As Cal began to get up, Kelly delivered a swift kick to his leg. "You forgot my bag!" she whispered.

While Cal preferred to escape with his life first in order to tell the story, he figured no one would believe him if he didn't have proof. He shimmied about halfway through before using his long arms to reach for Kelly's camera bag and pull it back with him.

As Cal was pulling the bag underneath the fence, one of the bag's elastic strings caught on the fence and caused the fence to clang as the string snapped free. The noise didn't go unnoticed.

"Over there!" one of the gunmen shouted.

"Go, Kelly, go!"

Cloverdale Industries maintained pristine landscaping. For this successful multi-level marketing company, no expense was too great to project the appearance of wealth. After all, that was the lure of drawing people in to sell their products. *Sell enough organic detergent, cleaners and liquid magnesium to your friends and you too can live in the lap of luxury.* That nauseating idea permeated Statenville, but it served Cal and Kelly at the moment.

The southwest corner of the property contained about an acre of densely wooded area thanks to a heavy irrigation effort by

Cloverdale. It provided ample cover for Cal and Kelly.

"When we get to the edge of these woods, we've got to sprint as fast as we can to the corner of the loading dock," Cal instructed. This wasn't his first time on the property. Cal covered Cloverdale Industries on a regular basis and was always making trips to the corporate headquarters to get the latest story.

"Got it," Kelly said.

They were near the edge of the woods and about 200 yards away from the unoccupied loading docks when Cal heard the chain link fence rattle. The gunmen were now on the property too.

Cal could hear the men furiously combing the area, yelling back and forth to one another. He was still terrified, but maintained a clear head about what he needed to do to keep Kelly safe. It was the only thing he could do. His adrenaline surged.

Cal pointed to Kelly where they were headed, choosing to remain silent. But it didn't matter.

"There they are!" one of the gunmen yelled, simultaneously taking off on a dead sprint.

Cal and Kelly didn't hesitate. They reached top speed in about 10 strides and didn't look back. . . until the shots rang out.

BANG! BANG!

Cal hit the ground.

CHAPTER 31

"WHY CAN'T ANYTHING EVER run smoothly around here?" Gold barked into the phone. "Call me when you've taken care of them."

"Yes, sir," responded the caller.

Running the city of Statenville was simple for Gold. He told people what to do and they did it. In a small town with a larger than average budget, it was easy.

Keeping the city's dark secret hidden was an intricate web of complexity. He continued to suppress his grief. Riley's death didn't come as a total shock to the Gold family. Nathan and his wife had known for a couple of months that Riley had begun dabbling in drugs, but they chose to ignore it. They never thought he would end up dead.

But that was the nature of Statenville's secret. It chose justification to assuage the town's collective conscience—the few who knew there was a secret to keep. Most people were oblivious to what was happening. Gold and his inner circle decided a long time ago to keep it that way. The fewer people who knew, the less chance a conscientious objector would one day come forward; that and the fact that they were all paid handsomely. Sometimes it meant blood was on their hands, but blood money didn't seem so bad when there was so much of it, enough to buy oneself a perfect life in Mayberry West.

Gold fingered a picture of Riley and stared out his office window. *Maybe this secret isn't worth it.* But then he looked around at what he had created, what Statenville was. It was costly, but it was most definitely worth it. Instead of becoming a virtual ghost town with a national failing economy, it was a boomtown. People were employed. They were happy. They were living a real dream. Did they really care where the money came from?

Those people never had a chance to decide if it was worth it. They never even knew. It was decided for them by Gold. They were but pawns in an elaborate get-rich scheme that was so flush with cash it opted to line the empty pockets of anyone who dared question them. It was much better than murdering them – and it raised less eyebrows than dead bodies. Everyone had a price. Almost everyone. There were always exceptions.

Cal Murphy had become an exception.

CHAPTER 32

GUY HUNG UP THE phone. Another grilling from Mr. Mendoza. Another order to tone down the coverage of the three teens' deaths in Wednesday's edition of *The Register*. Today, he truly felt like nothing more than a *managing* editor. No real decisions to make, just ensure people did what they were told.

It also explained why he was getting so agitated with Cal. With his assignment changed to a simple management position, Guy's star reporter was gone and not returning his calls. Guy couldn't even do the one thing he was being asked to do that day.

Three calls were made to Cal throughout the early afternoon. And three calls went straight to voicemail.

Guy had been tough on Cal before, but he always responded in a positive way. This time though, it wasn't elderly wisdom being passed down by Guy. It was a direct command, complete with all of Guy's redirected anger that went against every journalistic instinct Cal had ever cultivated. *Stop working on a story that could expose a deep level of corruption?* Cal had questioned after being told to stand down. And Guy knew it was a tough directive to follow. After all, stories like these were what journalists dreamed about at night while climbing into bed after eating a TV dinner all alone. At least, it was what Guy used to dream about.

Guy knew Cal would never stop pursuing this story. Something in the seasoned newspaperman's gut told him that Cal wasn't just concocting a cockamamie conspiracy theory. He only hoped Cal's pursuit of the truth wouldn't end in his death.

CHAPTER 33

CAL HEARD THE SHOT and felt the sting in his right arm almost simultaneously. He had never been shot before, nor had he imagined the searing pain that would accompany a bullet barreling into his tricep. It was such a sharp pain that it sent him sprawling toward the ground as he half tripped and half dove, hoping to avoid any other bullets whizzing his way.

Kelly dove for the ground as well. Lying on her stomach a few feet from Cal, she inched her way toward Cal while remaining on her belly. When she reached him, she frantically tried to get Cal to move. It was only about 15 yards to the dock, which had an open bay at the moment. With a gunfight breaking out, it was unlikely to stay open for long.

"Come on, Cal. We've got to move!"

Cal nodded, grimacing at the pain and the sight of blood gushing from his arm, despite pressure from his left hand. He looked more like a butcher than a reporter.

Two more bullets zipped in their direction, both off target.

Cal and Kelly scrambled for the open bay door. It took a few seconds for their eyes to adjust from the bright Idaho sunlight to the dimly lit warehouse space that was surprisingly less full than Cal anticipated. The back of the warehouse was empty and stretched into darkness for at least 300 yards. It was quickly looking like a dead end when it came to finding a place for cover.

Stacks of empty wooden pallets lined the back wall of the facility, and there was a small janitor's closet about 30 yards away.

Still no sign of anyone from inside the facility.

Cal recognized his two less-than-desirable choices: make a run for the racks and hide on top of a shelf, or hide in the janitor's closet. The burning sensation in Cal's arm along with the close proximity of the janitor's closet made Cal's decision easy.

* * *

Cloverdale security fanned out across the building looking for two suspects. Mel Davis, head of Cloverdale's security operation, received a phone call from one of the executives about a possible perimeter violation. A man and a woman were headed for their facility and they didn't have good intentions, at least that's what Davis was told.

The order was shoot to kill.

While he didn't mind the healthy paycheck, Mel often questioned why there was such tight security at a mid-level marketing company. Whenever he voiced his concern, he was silenced by the rehearsed chorus of managers telling him that corporate espionage is real—and if you don't take proactive steps to stop it, it will stop you.

Mel just nodded and did what he was told. This wasn't the first time he had shoot-to-kill orders, but he doubted he could pull the trigger if ever faced with one of these corporate spies.

* * *

From within the janitor's closet, Cal and Kelly heard the footsteps of presumed security guards racing around the building in search of them. They didn't dare speak, much less breathe.

They heard voices shouting out instructions about how they were going to sweep the facility. Then Cal heard something that lodged a lump in his throat. It was the phrase "shoot to kill."

He looked at Kelly, and, even in the darkness of a compact janitor's closet, he could see the terror in her eyes.

Cal had been careful not to bleed on the warehouse floor in order to prevent establishing an identifiable trail of blood. Kelly had added her left hand for additional pressure—and it seemed to be working at the moment.

Cal was itching to get something on his arm to clean out the wound and bandage it up. It didn't feel life threatening and he wasn't worried about it killing him. But he *was* worried about the untold number of armed security guards hunting them.

Most of the audible footsteps grew more distant. The search had apparently moved toward the other end of the facility. Cal and Kelly were almost feeling confident to breathe in a deep breath when slow-paced footsteps appeared to be headed straight for the janitor's closet.

Just then, Cal's iPhone buzzed. He scrambled to stop it. And then he and Kelly held their breaths. The footsteps had stopped. Right outside the closet door. Someone was blocking what little light had been seeping under the door. It was the only light Cal and Kelly had to faintly see anything in the closet. Sheer darkness matched sheer terror.

There was nothing. No movement. No sound. Just a pair of boots stationed outside the door and two occupants on the other side, holding their breath

Cal imagined the guard pressing his ear against the door and listening for any type of movement within. The pause at the door seemed to last an hour.

Then the guard jiggled the doorknob. Cal was glad he locked the door behind him but he knew this was probably the end. He cringed and prepared for the worst.

CHAPTER 34

"IT'S LOCKED," SHOUTED THE guard. "I don't hear anything. I don't see any blood either. And I don't feel like walking all the way back to our office just to get a key to double-check what I already know. Let's call this section of the warehouse clear and move on."

"I'm with you. Let's go," came the response.

The footsteps went from threatening to faint to gone. Cal and Kelly both felt it was safe to whisper but remained still.

"I thought we were done," Kelly said.

"And that was the first time you thought that today?" Cal's sarcasm attempted to lighten the gravity of the situation. It didn't work.

"No, but if we don't get you bandaged up and get out of here, someone *is* going to find us and turn us in."

It was five o'clock and Cal knew Guy would be looking for them. Maybe that was a good thing. Otherwise, who would be looking for them? As upset as Guy could get, his rage could cause him to send out a search party. As long as it wasn't the police, it would be OK.

Cal's phone vibrated. He had three missed calls and one text message. Guy hated text messaging, so Cal figured the calls were from his boss. He went to the text message. It was from Josh. In all the excitement over the past 48 hours, Cal nearly forgot Josh was coming to visit on Friday.

Looking fwd 2 seeing u & ragging u 4 starting Matt Garza on fantasy team. U r loyal 2 a fault. C u Thur

Checking his starting pitchers for his fantasy league team was the last thing on Cal's mind while stuck in a janitor's closet inside a building crawling with armed guards who were instructed to shoot him. But the text did cause Cal to smile and provided a momentary diversion from the fear beginning to take over his mind.

Cal then stood up and used the light from his iPhone to search for some strips of cloth to bandage his wound. By the dim light, Cal could tell that the wound wasn't nearly as deep as he initially thought. His arm still throbbed with sharp pain.

Kelly joined him, volunteering to shine the phone's light around the closet so Cal could thoroughly search the shelves for something to bandage him up. Cal found a first aid kit with some alcohol wipes to sterilize the wound along with some gauze and tape to dress it. Kelly took the items from Cal's hand. She began cleaning Cal's bloody arm and patching it up without the slightest communication from Cal. But she needed to talk.

"So how are we going to get out of here, Cal?"

Kelly's nerves were near their frazzled ends.

"Good question. I say we wait until it's dark and there's hardly anyone here. Then we try to hide in a delivery truck."

"A delivery truck? Are you out of your mind?"

Just then the sound of footsteps halted the hushed conversation. Four, maybe five people. Cal couldn't tell for sure. But they were within a few yards of the janitor's closet before they began talking. Cal and Kelly carefully returned to a sitting position.

"You guys be careful tonight. The boss man says there were some reporters who broke into our facility today. Do you all remember The Golden Rule? Let's play by it tonight. Got it?"

The remaining voices beyond the door muttered in agreement. They understood. Kelly thought she did too and gasped at the order before cupping her hand over her mouth. Cal scowled at her, something he knew Kelly could see even in the darkness of the closet.

"Peppy, you're headed to Seattle tonight. Big John, you're going to Portland. And Ringo, you've got the lucky all-nighter to San Francisco. As always, keep a low profile and travel the speed limit. We don't want anyone getting too interested in our product that shouldn't be ..."

"Product?" Cal faintly whispered. "I thought these people made vitamins and household cleaning supplies."

"... and remember, if you see those reporters, shoot to kill. We'll have a team clean up the mess and provide a nice cover story."

The footsteps sounded as if they headed out in different directions. Big overhead doors rolled up, breaking the still air. The hum of forklifts zipping about the warehouse overwhelmed the silence.

But it didn't matter to Cal. He still held his breath, hoping Kelly was doing the same. Maybe he wasn't that interested in writing this story after all. If the teens were dead, the teens were dead. No amount of sleuthing could bring them back. But Cal had already dug too far. Now all these Cloverdale Industries goons were concerned with was silencing him and Kelly – permanently. Yet the story was getting more intricate and dangerous to Cal. It appeared that Cloverdale Industries was involved in a different type of multi-level marketing company—and it wasn't legal.

CHAPTER 35

GUY SLAMMED HIS PHONE down and let out another string of expletives. Two hours until deadline and his two best newsroom personnel had vanished. Between Cal and Kelly's phones, Guy had left six messages and didn't get a single response. He even sent Mindy over to Cal's apartment to look for them, and he hadn't heard from her in nearly an hour. His newsroom was falling apart with two hours to go before deadline.

But Guy didn't really care about their big story, although he was sure their pursuit of it had something to do with all of Cal's recent questionable behavior. All he wanted were two warm bodies writing articles and editing photos. This legendary gunslinger in the newsroom was turning his back on his arch nemesis – hard news. He was too tired to fight political battles and public perception. He just hoped that if he turned his back, no shots would be fired. It was time to ride off into the sunset and be a good newspaper man for a small community paper, where scandals surface on the next-to-last page at the bottom in the briefs section—if at all.

The voices in his head fought courageously.

"What's your gut telling you, Guy?"

"It's telling me that I'm going to get another ulcer worrying about this story."

"Don't you want to know the truth."

"Sure, but nobody else here does. Why make any waves?"

"What's happened to you, man? You used to stand for something."

"I am standing for something—my sanity ... and my job. There's no need to mess with a good thing."

And Guy settled it—for now. Just get those trouble-making reporters back into the office and put this week's paper to bed. That would make this all go away right now. If only he knew where Cal and Kelly were, he would go get them himself.

Guy sat down at his desk, burying his head in his hands. He let out a long sigh. The powder keg was set to blow.

***

Joseph Mendoza looked across the office into *The Register*'s newsroom from his publisher's perch—the only walled office in the building. He used to care about the truth at one point too. But not anymore. It didn't pay nearly as well as the lies.

His office phone buzzed. It was Gold.

"Hello, Mr. Mayor. Any news to report?"

"That's why I called you. Don't you run a little thing called the *news*paper? Besides, it's your employees that are mucking everything up."

"They won't be employed here any longer. As soon as I find them, they're gone."

"Even your niece?"

"Especially her. She still thinks she's going to get this paper—and there's not a snowball's chance in hell that I would give it to her."

"Well, I applaud your resolve to do whatever it takes ..." Gold's voice trailed off. He paused. Then he restarted his sentence, pushing the limits of acceptable decibel levels. "... BUT IT'S NOT GOOD ENOUGH! FIND YOUR EMPLOYEES OR ELSE SUFFER THE CONSEQUENCES!"

Yelling rarely rattled Mendoza. For someone coming from a lineage of impassioned Basque people, yelling merely revealed that one was unsatisfied with something. It didn't usually convey the same urgency as someone outside his family might express. Gold was outside Mendoza's family.

Mendoza shook as he hung up the phone, thoroughly frightened at the way Gold was growing more paranoid by the hour. It was traumatic enough that Gold had lost his son two days before, but to have his very way of life threatened? He wasn't going to let this pass without doing some damage. Mendoza realized he wasn't collateral either—he would be in the crosshairs if things didn't go Gold's way. His reporters' whereabouts suddenly became his chief concern.

* * *

Still seething in his own right about the apparent abandonment of his two best news people, Guy might have accepted the order with welcome arms. Mendoza had just called him to say that Cal and Kelly were to be fired immediately—or whenever he saw them next.

Instead of gladly accepting this order to rid himself of the two biggest pains in his life over the past two days, Guy – the newspaper man gunslinger – stopped to think. Was his complicity in Statenville's secret going to result in the death of both a reporter and photographer he had grown fond of? Was a sack full of money on his back porch every month worth having their blood on his hands? He was unsure of what his next step should be, even though he knew which one he preferred to take.

Guy also knew diplomacy was the key to surviving long enough to deliver the final editorial blow, if that's the direction he decided to choose. In the meantime, he would have to seethe in private about granting permission to have his editorial power stripped.

CHAPTER 36

KELLY INCHED CLOSER TO Cal, serving the two-fold purpose of calming her terror and putting pressure on his wound. Cal pulled her even closer.

"We're going to be OK, Kelly, but you've got to hold it together. If these guys hear us, we're done."

Kelly quietly sniffled as she nodded. They both knew what was at stake—and it was far more than winning some writing award that seemed rather trivial considering the new ante.

For more than 30 minutes, Cal and Kelly sat motionless as the warehouse whirred with the sound of normal commerce. Every sound of approaching and fading footsteps created a series of emotional highs and lows for them. Would this be the moment someone would discover them before putting a few bullets in their defenseless bodies? Despite all the near misses, nobody seemed concerned with mopping the floor at the moment. What mattered was getting those mysterious deliveries out the door and onto their destinations.

Finally, the last audible footsteps faded and it was quiet again.

Cal was curious—and impatient. He pressed his face flat against the cold concrete floor and squinted one eye closed. With his other eye, he peered into the warehouse, looking for feet. He saw none. But he did see a stack of boxes just 10 feet outside the janitor's closet.

Without a warning to Kelly, he jumped up and dashed out the door, grabbed a small box with a Cloverdale Industries logo imprinted on the side and ran back to the closet, re-securing the door.

"Are you nuts?!" Kelly shouted in a whisper.

"Yes, I am. But if these goons are gonna kill us, at least I want to know why."

Cal took out his house keys and slid it across the tape that held the box together. Except for his moment of insanity, he had been careful to do everything as quietly as possible.

He opened the box and pulled out the packing material. Inside the box was a bottle of "Clean and Clear." Instead of containing a cleaning liquid, it was filled with white crystals.

"That doesn't look clean to me," Cal whispered, shining the light of his cell phone on the foreign substance.

"It's not," Kelly said. "It looks like crystal meth."

Cal attended plenty of wild college parties in his day, but he never stuck around long enough to see any drug usage beyond guys smoking weed. It was the first time he had seen it, much less held enough to guarantee him a 20-year prison sentence if a cop walked in on him now.

"What is this place, Kelly?"

"I've heard rumors but nobody ever told me anything for sure."

"Rumors of what?"

"Oh, crazy stuff, like what you might hear at a sleepover party."

"Like what?!" Cal was growing impatient and nearly let his voice rise above a whisper.

"OK, OK. I've heard a couple of times that Cloverdale Industries produces all these cleaning products and vitamins as a cover for its drug operation."

"Drug operation?"

"Yeah, I haven't heard much other than that. You know, kids talking in middle school. I never really believed it. I've got relatives who work here. They're not those kind of people."

"Well, I've got a bottle of crystal meth that says your middle school pajama parties revealed something more than who had a crush on Bobby Jackson."

"Bobby Jackson?"

"Every school has a dreamy Bobby Jackson, right? Oh, forget it. The point is, I've got evidence in my hand that this is indeed *some* type of drug operation. Now, we need you to take a picture to give us some evidence to take back that isn't going to get me thrown in jail for the most promising years of my career."

"You want me to take a picture?"

"Yes. Just get out your camera. I'll pour this on the floor and you can take a picture with the bottle."

"Cal, that's not going to prove anything."

"Maybe not, but it might be enough to get the feds interested in investigating what's going on here."

Cal turned the light on and Kelly snapped a couple of pictures. Then back to darkness. Cal returned the contents to the bottle and was about to repackage the box when the sound of heavy footsteps began getting closer. This time, it didn't sound like it was somebody who was going to pass by.

The footsteps stopped just short of the door. The clinging of what was undoubtedly a large keychain sounded like the chambering of a bullet to Cal and Kelly. They both held their breath. Cal didn't think it mattered as he was convinced his heartbeat was audible.

A key slid into the lock. The doorknob turned.

CHAPTER 37

ONLY 90 MINUTES UNTIL press time for *The Register*. Guy paced in his tight office space, trying to digest the news Mindy had just delivered.

She returned to the office 20 minutes before and gave Guy a full report. It was so thorough and marked with details that he wondered if she might be interested in being a reporter. After all, he was about to have an opening. Her work in gathering information at Cal's apartment was a full three pay grades above making coffee.

When Mindy arrived at Cal's apartment, she found Kelly's car in the parking lot with two smashed in side windows. Broken glass littered the adjacent empty parking spaces.

Cal's front door was wide open. The wood around the door handle splintered in several directions. Even the back door was open. And in between? Chaos.

Books, newspapers and magazines strewn across the floor. Chairs lying on their side. A smashed TV, likely as a parting gesture of good will. Cabinets were open. Smashed dishes covered the kitchen floor.

"Cal? Kelly? Are you guys here?" Mindy timidly called, hoping to not hear a sound as she maneuvered through the wreckage. She didn't.

She ventured upstairs and saw more of the same. It was as if Cal's bachelor pad had developed a stomach bug and vomited. At least she hoped the second floor was the work of intruders and not an indication of Cal's sloppy housekeeping.

After Mindy swept through the house to ensure there wasn't a clue for where Cal and Kelly might have gone, she found nothing that made much sense. Only an open shed door and what appeared to be fresh black motorcycle tracks on the neighboring patio. But there was nothing definitively linking the two.

Guy felt helpless. He wanted to help out his reporters but had no idea what to do. The sheriff's deputies sure weren't going to offer any help. And at this point, for all Guy knew, they were the ones who did this to Cal and Kelly. But he had no idea where to start to help. The best thing he could do was stay in his office and get out this week's edition of *The Register*. If he lost his job, he might lose his credibility. He would likely be dismissed as a disgruntled employee trying to find a way to get back at his employer. That would all make finding an outlet to run Cal's story all the more challenging.

So he sat at his desk and continued editing. And prayed.

CHAPTER 38

CAL FELT KELLY'S GRIP tighten on his arms as they both cringed. This was it. No time for bravado. Only an immediate plea for mercy.

The door swung open and a hand groped the wall for the light switch.

Click!

"Cal? Kelly?" asked the whispering voice in bewilderment. "What are you doing in here?"

They both looked up to see a familiar friendly face: Buddy Walker, the Statenville High boys basketball coach.

"What are *you* doing here?" Cal whispered back as he inspected Walker's blue jumpsuit with his name stitched into his left chest panel.

Walker stepped inside and shut the door. He hung his head.

"To be frank, I don't make enough money at the school, so I've been moonlighting as a janitor. It's terribly embarrassing. Please don't tell anyone, OK?"

"Don't worry, Coach. I won't tell a soul."

"Me either," piped Kelly.

"Thanks, guys. That would mean a lot to me. My mother is sick and feeble – and I'm trying to take care of her. It's not something I can easily do on a teacher's salary in the middle-of-nowhere

Idaho."

"Don't be embarrassed, Coach. What you're doing is very noble," Kelly said.

Before things turned too mushy, Cal knew they only had a limited amount of time to regroup and focus on escaping the facility without being seen.

"Look, Coach. We're in a bit of a predicament and need your help."

"What happened to your arm? And again, what are you doing in this closet?" Coach Walker asked, suddenly awakening to the abnormality of the situation.

"It's simple: we need to get out of here without anyone seeing us. If I told you everything, you'd think we were crazy. "

"Try me."

"OK, here it goes. We're being pursued by some type of secret government agents and we know some powerful people who own this facility want us dead, too. The security guards here have orders to kill us on sight if they see us."

Coach Walker stared at Cal and said nothing.

"I swear it's true. I couldn't make this stuff up."

Finally, he asked the question Cal hadn't really pondered.

"Why do they care about you, Cal? What do you know?"

"Well, I know enough to gain the interest of some government investigation group."

"Like what?"

"Like, this facility is a commercial drug operation that uses its cover as a muti-level marketing company to hide a drug distribution network."

"OK, you're right. I don't believe you."

"Please, Coach Walker. You've got to believe me. See, look at this meth I found."

Cal showed Walker some of the drugs he had found, which was enough to elicit an eyebrow raise from the coach moonlighting as a janitor.

"Well, I did see some armed security guards running around, but I'm not ready to believe all your tin hat theories."

"Fine. I don't care if you believe those. I just need your to help us escape."

Coach Walker stroked his jaw and appeared to be deep in thought. Finally, after a long pause, he spoke.

"Honestly, I don't believe you, but it's stranger than strange that you're hiding in the janitor closet and security appears to be heightened at the moment. I've got a 15-minute break coming up. I can probably get you to my house that's five minutes away—and in time for me to get back to work without missing my window to punch back in."

Cal wanted to hug Walker, but he figured the pain he would suffer in his arm wouldn't be worth it.

"Wait here and I'll be back in five minutes with a cart for you to hide in. I'll push you out and then you can get into the backseat of my car. I don't think you'll be noticed. I've got a blanket you can cover up with once you're on the floorboard."

"Sounds good."

Walker flipped the light switch as he exited the closet and locked the door behind him.

Five minutes later, the squeaky wheel of a large commercial dirty clothes cart could be heard rolling in their direction.

Walker whispered, "It's me, guys," just before he unlocked the door. Then he opened it and moved the cart up to the opening so Cal and Kelly could climb in. They curled up in a fetal position and put their heads down as Walker draped a blanket over them. He wheeled the pair to his silver Subaru Forester and helped them scramble inside. Cal would have preferred the ability to see Kelly's face during the ride to Walker's house, especially since he was so close to her. But in a day of near misses and running for his life, Cal would settle for huddling in the darkness beneath a blanket with Kelly.

Walker's plan was executed to perfection. He returned the dirty clothes cart to just inside the rollup door at the top of the dock and walked back to the car.

"Thanks, Coach," Cal whispered from beneath the blanket. "We really appreciate this. You might have saved our lives."

Through the vibrations in the floorboard, Cal felt the gears clicking into place as Walker jammed the stick into reverse.

"Oh, it's not a big deal, Cal. I'm sure you'd do the same for me."

"Of course," came Cal's muffled voice from under the blanket.

***

Walker smiled as he shifted his car back into the drive position with his right hand. His left hand fingered his gun.

Cal and Kelly had eluded him all day. *Could it really be this easy?*

CHAPTER 39

BENEATH THE BLANKET, CAL pulled out his iPhone and quietly began texting Guy. He knew it was risky, but without anyone else to trust in the whole town, he felt like maybe Guy could help him out.

Look up Coach Walker's address & meet us there in 1 hr

Cal looked up at Kelly and smiled. He then typed a short message into a notes program:

We're going 2 b ok.

***

Guy's cell phone vibrated across his desk, alerting him to the arrival of a message. It was Cal.

Guy was overjoyed at the fact that Cal and Kelly seemed to be alive and OK. But meeting them anywhere in an hour was impossible with press time nearing. He typed off a quick text to Cal and shut his phone.

His anger had been replaced by relief and joy. Then his mind went to thinking about what this story that was rocking Statenville was really all about. Drugs? Power? Money? Revenge? He hoped Cal had some answers. If Guy was going to leave, he wanted to do it big, just like he had in Salt Lake City when he revealed the bribery of Olympic Committee members in order to secure the host selection for the Winter Olympics. Nothing like lighting a powder keg and walking away.

Guy had already begun plotting how he would do it this time. All he needed were Cal's notes.

His desk phone rang. He knew what it meant: time to start press checking the special insert section. He left his office without answering the phone.

***

With almost every news staff member buried in their work and all the rest of the paper's marketing, sales and circulation personnel gone for the day, Sammy figured nobody would notice him sneaking into the boss's office. He was right.

Sammy looked through Guy's recent calls list and saw nothing. Then he switched to the list of text messages, opening Cal's most recent one at the top. He closed the phone and headed to the break room.

Mr. Gold would not be happy about this, but at least all his problems were gathering in one place.

CHAPTER 40

ON THE SHORT RIDE to Walker's house, Cal kept running through all the scenarios of why a government agency might be interested in keeping word of this drug operation from getting out. *Was the government mounting a case against the company? Were there other people involved that he didn't know about? How many people* did *know about this operation? Why go all cloak and dagger on him?*

He knew that Sheriff Jones and some of his deputies were at the very least on the take. So, there were some people who seemed highly interested in making sure this information never saw wet ink on printing press. Just how far did this cover up go? Cal's mind seemed to be stuck in a perpetual eight-figure, unable to advance any ideas in a meaningful way. His head began to hurt trying to hash out all the possibilities.

At the moment, all he knew was that he was thankful for Walker's fortuitous timing. Without his intervention, who knows if he and Kelly would've ever made it out of Cloverdale Industries alive. He didn't want to think about the grim possible outcomes.

Ten minutes had passed since they left Cloverdale. Cal thought Walker obviously lived much farther away than he claimed to live.

Just then, the car came slowed to a stop and Cal heard what sounded like a large door opening, but it didn't seem like any garage door he had ever heard. *What is going on?*

"We're heeere!" Walker said in a cheery sing-song voice.

* * *

Guy sat down at his desk and exhaled, rubbing his temples. "Forget it," he muttered to himself. With the press check still 45 minutes away, Guy felt uneasy about leaving Cal and Kelly unexposed for so long. Besides, no one would suspect him. He could aid and abet Cal all he wanted. Who would be the wiser?

"Sammy, get in my office," Guy bellowed.

Sammy hung up on his call and scurried from the break room into Guy's office.

"What is it, boss?"

"Sammy, I think it's about time you take on some more responsibility. Tonight, I'm putting you in charge of press check. You just reread all the headlines and stories once the first few papers come off the press and make sure Terry didn't screw up any headlines or sneak some filthy double entendre in there. You think you can handle that?"

"Sure."

"All right. Great. I'm out of here. You're in charge, Sammy. Have fun."

"Where you going, boss? Got a hot date?"

Guy shot Sammy a disgusted look.

"Don't worry about my love life. You worry about making sure the paper comes out right. Got it?"

Guy didn't wait for a response. He kept walking toward the back door without looking back.

CHAPTER 41

WHEN WALKER'S CAR STOPPED, Cal began to get an uneasy feeling about his getaway chauffeur. Walker seemed way too willing to help out when a more rational response would have been to report their whereabouts to his superior. And maybe he did. But at the moment, Cal felt like he had been tricked.

Before he had any more time to ponder if bumping into Walker had been fortuitous or staged, both doors to the backseat flung open at once. Cal heard Kelly struggling and shouting at whoever was pulling her out of the car. Cal, more concerned with Kelly's well-being, protested as well. But the blanket wasn't even fully off his head before he felt Walker slide a needle into his neck.

Cal slumped to the floor.

***

Walker and his colleague dragged Cal and Kelly into the same room where Cal had been held less than 24 hours ago. This time, they needed another chair.

"You better hurry," the other man said. "You don't have much time."

Walker didn't say a word. He just kept wrapping the limp bodies of Cal and Kelly to the chairs that were positioned back to back. No need to take any chances by putting them next to each other. Walker's colleague sealed their mouths shut with duct tape.

Walker stood at the doorway and smiled at his good fortune: the pesky reporter who refused to heed his warnings and his sidekick were now his temporary guests. He watched the unsettled dust hang in the air before turning off the light. They would forgive his rude treatment later. They would understand. Everyone understood the importance of protecting the common good. Even meddlesome reporters.

* * *

Guy was fumbling for his car keys in his briefcase when Sheriff Jones roared into *The Register*'s parking lot and parked at an angle behind Guy. There was no way Guy could maneuver his white 2009 Cadillac CTS Coupe out of his parking space now.

Jones took his time getting out of his car. He didn't appear to be in a hurry. Guy was.

"Hi, Sheriff. What's the meaning of all this?"

"Well, I thought you could tell me, Guy."

"I'm sorry?"

"Where are you going in such a hurry?"

"I think I asked you a question first."

"Are you getting smart with me, Mr. Newspaper Man?"

"Nope. Just wanting to know why you came flying into the parking lot here just to block my car in."

"You've got a busted taillight and I didn't want you to get a ticket."

"A busted tail light?" Guy began to walk around to the back of the car to verify Jones's claim. He didn't see anything that resembled a scratched taillight, much less a busted one. "What are you talking about?"

"I'm talking about this one."

With that statement, Jones pulled his foot back and kicked the left taillight with his boot heel, causing the plastic to crack and splinter.

"You better be careful not to get on the road with that light busted like it is."

Guy couldn't believe what he just witnessed. He had heard from some people in the community that Jones could be ruthless. Hearing about it and watching it happen were two different things. Guy never imagined Jones would abuse his authority to that degree.

"I'd get that fixed if I were you," Jones said, scribbling out a busted tail light warning for Guy.

Guy began to protest.

"Who do you think you—"

"No, no, no, Guy. You know who I am and you know who I think I am—and they are the same person. I'm the same person who can take you to jail for driving with a busted taillight. So, I suggest you get Carson down at the auto parts shop to get you a new one before you get back on the road and I have to take you in."

"*Jail?* For a busted taillight?"

"I don't make the laws, Guy. I just enforce 'em."

Jones climbed back into his car and rolled down the driver's side window for a parting salvo.

"I'll be watching you, Guy."

Guy looked at the warning ticket in his hand as Jones drove off. There wasn't anything he could do to help Cal and Kelly now—except walk to the auto parts store and pick out a new taillight.

Guy hammered out a short text explaining the reason for his delay and began walking toward Hal's Auto Parts Store one block down from *The Register*. He knew time was the commodity that mattered most when it came to helping Cal, but Jones had just shortened his supply of it.

CHAPTER 42

DAWKINS' PATROL CAR ZOOMED up the driveway of Walker's house. Only five minutes before, Dawkins and rookie deputy Willie Warren had been attacking a plate of ribs from Ray-Ray's when Sheriff Jones radioed for them to check out a disturbance at the Walker place.

After Dawkins was in the car, Sheriff Jones called him on his cell to let him know that the "disturbance" was actually the location of Statenville's hottest fugitive, Cal Murphy. The sheriff was tipped off to Cal and Kelly's whereabouts and the two snoopy reporters were about to be arrested on more trumped up charges.

Without any reason to believe the situation was dangerous, Dawkins took his time getting out of his car. He sent Warren around the back of the house to make sure the elusive reporters didn't make an attempt to escape. Lacking familiarity with Cal and Kelly, Warren unholstered his gun. He wanted the two fugitives to know he was serious.

Meanwhile, Dawkins sauntered up to the door and rang the doorbell. Then he waited. If anyone was home, they weren't moving about the house. Silence ruled the air.

"I know you're in there, Cal," Dawkins yelled. "Don't make this any more difficult than it has to be."

No response.

Dawkins began pounding on the front door.

***

When the sedative wore off, Cal guessed it hadn't been that long, but he couldn't be sure. Sitting in a pitch black room fastened to a chair with your mouth taped shut offered few ways to get any answers—if there was anyone else in the room to get answers from.

He grunted as he tried to shout Kelly's name. Nothing.

With no light, he couldn't see if she was even in the room, much less if she was all right. Cal figured with Kelly's smaller frame, she would take a little longer to awaken from the sedative. But Cal knew she was there. He could smell her. All day the sweet smell of her perfume had reminded him that the thrill ride they were on had become more about protecting her than extracting the truth from a well-guarded mystery.

After doing nothing but sitting in the dark and trying to piece together the disjointed events of the day, Cal felt Kelly begin to stir.

She began her muffled cries for help, too.

Cal responded with a few of his own.

The pointless exchange went on for about a minute until they both realized communicating was impossible without the ability to make a cognitive sound. Being bound to a chair back to back in a dark room didn't help either.

They went five minutes without even a grunt or a stir coming from either one. Cal decided not to fight Walker either. It was clear that pleas for mercy were more helpful than lecturing him for the mistreatment. Cal still wasn't sure what Walker was doing, but he concluded that his interest was in removing him temporarily from this investigation rather than doing bodily harm. The chances were aplenty to do that, but Walker continued to side with mercy over murder. This, too, puzzled Cal.

Only the occasional scuffle of feet moving outside the door broke the silence.

Until Cal and Kelly heard someone pounding on an exterior door.

Immediately, the room filled with muffled screams from the immobile reporters. The voice that accompanied the pounding on the door was a familiar one.

CHAPTER 43

DAWKINS GREW TIRED OF waiting. He knew Warren might do something stupid if the tension continued to build. Just as he resolved that he was going to get the battering ram out of his car and pull Cal and Kelly from the house, Dawkins heard muffled screams. It sounded like someone was in the house.

Dawkins ran to his patrol car and popped the trunk to retrieve the battering ram. He yelled for Warren to join him in the front. Warren came scrambling around the side of the house.

"What is it, Dawkins? What's going on?"

"I heard some screams coming from the house, so whoever is in there may not be voluntarily. We're going to have to bust the door down and find out what's going on. You ready?"

"What do you want me to do?"

"Just stand back here and cover me while I knock the door down. Then follow me in and be ready for anything. Got it?"

"Yep. Let's do it."

"OK. Stand back."

Dawkins needed three heaving blasts from the battering ram to bust open the door. He dropped it and rushed into the house, drawing his weapon in case he met any strong resistance. Warren followed. He handled the gun as if it was the first time he had been in a potential combative situation since becoming a deputy – because it was his first time.

The muffled screams hadn't stopped since Dawkins first heard them. For two straight minutes he had heard what sounded like pleas for help. Dawkins and Warren raced down the hall on the left side of the house, looking for a room that might contain the voices. No luck. Then the right side. Nothing there either.

Warren froze and looked down.

"I think it's coming from the basement."

Dawkins nodded.

"Good work, rook."

Dawkins located the door to the stairs and flipped on the light switch. The cries continued as they rushed down the stairs. They were getting louder.

The basement was unfinished. The lighting was roughed in, as were some of the walls. It didn't even have a cement floor in some parts, as dirt served that function.

As Dawkins and Warren crept through the empty space, they located a single door in the back corner of the room. The cries were coming from there.

Dawkins jammed his shoulder against the wall just outside the door. He looked at Warren, who had taken up a position across from him by the door.

"You ready?" Dawkins whispered.

"Let's do it."

Dawkins flung open the door.

***

Cal and Kelly agonized over their potential savior. The person who was about to walk through the door could either be a friend or foe. But in either case, their situation was about to change.

They never stopped screaming for help, even beneath sealed lips.

Finally, a light pierced the room's darkness, giving Cal a better idea of his situation. Until that moment, all he knew was that he was bound to a chair on a dirt floor with Kelly behind him. But room dimensions or other objects in the room? Cal had no idea about the true nature of his environment.

Despite a strong desire to get out of his chair, Cal's anxiety heightened with each passing second. What if their savior wasn't really a savior? What if he was more like a tormentor? He cringed.

The door sprang open.

CHAPTER 44

DAWKINS SQUINTED AS HE peered into the room. It took a moment for his eyes to adjust to the darkness as he felt around for a light switch. He finally found one and flicked it on. The man lying on the floor looked unfamiliar to him.

The man squirmed around, attempting to say something but to no avail as the duct tape over his mouth suppressed any potential successful communication.

Dawkins knelt down beside the man, whose hands were fastened behind his back with duct tape as were his feet.

"Who are you? And what are you doing here?"

Dawkins ripped the duct tape off the man's mouth.

"I'm special agent Chris Cooper from the FBI. Help me up!"

Dawkins flashed a wry smile at the moment only he would find comedic. Then he got serious.

"Not until you answer my second question."

"What does it look like I'm doing? I'm squirming on the floor trying to convince Barney Fife to help me out."

"You're a funny man, Agent Cooper. I always thought Barney Fife would be the one squirming on the floor, duped by someone else—not the one in charge of the situation."

Cooper's biting edge softened. "Just help me up, OK?"

"I want some answers first."

"I don't really have any for you. I'm here handling an internal situation."

"It doesn't look like you're handling it very well."

"Enough with the wise cracks. Just get me untied, OK?"

Dawkins and Warren began freeing Cooper, who didn't demonstrate much gratitude once he was on his feet.

Despite the runaround Cooper gave him, Dawkins was determined to get some more answers.

"Let me see your badge, Agent Cooper."

Cooper dug into his pocket and pulled out an official FBI badge.

Satisfied with Cooper's credential, Dawkins pressed on.

"Do you know Buddy Walker?"

"I already told you that I'm not at liberty to say anything. I'm only here handling an internal matter."

"Well, we got a tip that Walker was holding someone hostage, which is why I'm even here saving your sorry self. So, if your Walker is that internal matter you're talking about, I'll be happy to let it remain your problem and drop our investigation. Otherwise, I'm going to make your life miserable. So, what's it gonna be?"

"I'm sorry, but I can't tell you anything else. Now, if you'll excuse me, I need to get going."

Cooper headed toward the basement stairs with Dawkins right behind him.

"Great. I'm sure Judge Johnson won't mind issuing a search warrant for Walker's house, seeing that we have plenty of probable cause—and the fact that the Judge is my uncle."

Cooper stopped his march up the basement stairs.

"Look. Please don't start causing any trouble. You have no idea who you're messing with. If you jeopardize this operation, I have my own ways of dealing with you. And I promise you won't like them."

Dawkins bowed up.

"Is that a threat? Because you're in my town now, not some big fancy city where the FBI walks all over local law enforcement. We're the law here."

"It's your grave, Barney."

Cooper chose to make that his parting salvo and continued ascending the basement stairs.

Dawkins made his final appeal, which came out more like a threat.

"Boy, it would be a shame, Agent Cooper, if you got arrested for trespassing."

Cooper didn't look back as he reached the top step and opened the door. He began sprinting for the front door.

"Let's go," Dawkins said to Warren as they scrambled after Cooper.

By the time Dawkins and Warren made it to the front yard, all they saw were the taillights on Cooper's Cadillac Escalade.

Dawkins kicked the ground in disgust. Cooper's arrogance grated on his last nerve. He had untied Cooper only to be mocked, lied to and humiliated.

But Dawkins didn't really need a definitive answer from Cooper. He was no Barney Fife. He now knew that Walker was a federal agent, too.

CHAPTER 45

WHILE ON THE RUN since lunch, Cal feared his next encounter with Guy. But when he saw Guy's face after he busted through the door, feelings of terror gave way to relief.

Guy ran over to his only two staffers worth more than a pile of two-day-old newsprint and ripped the duct tape off their mouths.

"Thank God you found us!" Cal said. He hugged Guy, who never looked like he wanted a hug—and still didn't in this tense moment.

"Enough with the mushy gratitude. What have you two have gotten yourselves into?"

"We're still trying to figure it all out," Cal said.

"Tell me what you know so far, starting with why you're in Buddy Walker's barn."

"We're in Buddy Walker's barn?" Kelly asked what Cal was thinking.

"I once considered buying this property when it was up for sale three years ago. Ten secluded acres on the edge of town. What's not to love? I remember this place well, so I just figured if something shady went down, it would happen out here. You can't see this structure from the house. Besides, I saw Dawkins' squad car at the house when I drove by."

"Dawkins? Here?"

"He was when I drove by, but he's a worthless deputy and wouldn't think of checking here. But talk fast just in case."

Cal wasted no time in recounting the events of the past six hours in efficient broad strokes. Regurgitating the who, what, when, where and why for every school board meeting and middle school girls basketball games enabled him to spell out the big picture without wasting words. He figured since Guy was a newspaper man, he could fill in the blanks himself.

Just as Cal was about to tell Guy about finding crystal meth at the Cloverdale plant, he stopped.

"What is this place?" he asked.

Lost in the excitement over their rescue, Cal and Kelly had hardly noticed their surroundings. Guy's revelation that they were in Walker's barn satisfied their initial curiosity to their whereabouts. They didn't even inspect the room.

The room was a sizable 20 feet by 20 feet, likely a large tack room at one point. With dirt floors and wooden walls, the décor was rustic. A mirror framed in an old saddle hung on the far wall, a relic that probably survived from the property's previous owner. But it wasn't the mirror that arrested Cal's attention. It was the out-of-place dry erase boards.

Each wall had at least two boards with chemical equations scribbled all over them. It looked like gibberish to Cal. He hated organic chemistry. Equations and rudimentary molecular structures appeared like ancient hieroglyphics. *What did all of this mean?*

While Cal stood staring at the board, he hoped something from that class would come back to him. It didn't. Fortunately, he wasn't the only one in the room.

"Uh, Cal, this is big stuff," Kelly said. She stood slack jawed, staring at the boards and awaiting Cal's response.

"I was hoping either you or Guy would know what this is, because I don't remember a thing from college chemistry class."

"This is really big stuff, Cal."

Cal was growing annoyed with Kelly's foreboding and redundant statements.

"Spit it out, Kelly!"

"I think I might know how those kids died."

"What? They overdosed on drugs?"

"Nope. It probably wasn't an overdose—and it wasn't an accident either."

CHAPTER 46

GOLD HATED FEELING OUT of control, yet at this moment, it was as if his hands were tied behind his back while in the driver's seat of a speeding sports car headed for a 45-degree turn. Off-road danger was imminent. Could he survive?

Statenville had survived plenty of scares under his watch. New snooping citizens. Disgruntled employees. Curious trespassers. They could all be persuaded. Brandish a handgun or flash some cash—whatever the situation called for. In most situations, the person developed an immediate case of amnesia. There was an unused rocky quarry in a secluded canyon for everyone else.

But a federal agent? Working at Cloverdale Industries? With access to every room? This was far beyond a simple breach.

Gold had implemented rigorous "background checks" for all new employees. He even checked his current employees at the time. Everyone understood the sacred secret that they kept. Should it get out, it not only meant that they lost their healthy paychecks, but they would also likely go to federal prison for a long time. He underscored the serious nature of their "business" every opportunity he had at closed corporate gatherings. But Walker, the innocent basketball coach needing a few hours to help support his elderly mother, passed his background check without as much as a raised eyebrow. He had a few run-ins with the law, but nothing out of the ordinary. Nothing to make Gold suspect Walker wasn't who he claimed to be.

Yet Gold's failsafe had been eluded and now he was dealing with his nightmare scenario. Not only that, but Walker had been working with another agent. How much the other agent knew was a wild card. If they were really working together, Walker wouldn't have likely tied him up. At this point, Gold had to take a risk. Without one, life as he had crafted it for the good people of Statenville would be gone forever. One misstep and Statenville would turn into a rural ghost town like every other small town in America that hadn't figured out a way to beat the gloomy economic times. But Gold only told himself that to assuage his conscience. He knew it was never really about Statenville or its people.

He took a deep breath. Hyperventilating wouldn't allow him to think clearly.

Then he stopped and smiled. It was in moments like these that he patted himself on the back for adding every local law enforcement personnel to the Cloverdale Industries payroll. It was strictly a cash payroll with laundered money hand delivered weekly in an unmarked envelope. It bought Gold the extra help he needed when he needed it.

Right now, he needed it more than ever.

***

Walker sped toward Cloverdale Industries. His long deep-cover assignment was almost over. It would already be over if Cooper had his way. Not everyone at the FBI's Salt Lake field office agreed with Walker's tactics. In fact, most people didn't. Going off script and using unorthodox – and at times, illegal – methods to achieve his assignment didn't make him popular.

But when Cooper showed up and began leveling career-ending accusations, Walker knew he had to overstep protocol bounds to get the job done. He wanted out of the hellhole he referred to as Statenville. And if he had his way, every TV station with a news crew within 500 miles would descend upon this podunk town and cover the story of the year. He didn't care that he would never get any credit for single-handedly taking down the Northwest's biggest drug cartel. His just reward would be seeing the Statenville city limits sign vanish in his rearview mirror never to be seen with his own two eyes ever again.

However, there was still plenty of work remaining in order to get released from his assignment.

Code Enfuego for Buddy Walker!

His scanner, tuned into the local sheriff's office, squawked an esoteric code as well as a brief description of Walker and his car from a dispatcher.

It was in moments like these that he reveled in the fact that Elliott Mercer was sitting right next to him in the passenger's seat.

CHAPTER 47

KELLY STARED AT THE formulas surrounding her on the walls of Walker's research lab and occasional prison. She snapped a photo of each picture with her iPhone and emailed them to her personal account.

"What is it?" Cal demanded, growing impatient with Kelly's cryptic response and behavior.

"I think Walker was meddling with crystal meth by adding some interesting chemicals."

"Chemicals that would kill someone?" Guy asked, trying to keep up.

"It doesn't look like it, but chemicals are a fickle thing. If he added too much of one thing, it could create a different reaction than he anticipated."

"Like scratching yourself to death?" Cal asked.

"Maybe. I need to study this a little bit more to figure out exactly what he was trying to do and look up some side effects of these drugs. But that's my working theory."

"Scratching yourself to death? What are you talking about, Kelly?" Guy had abandoned all ideas of self-preservation. He couldn't resist a hard news story that included murder and government cover-ups. Guy was all in.

"Cal, show him those pictures."

Cal called up the series of photos he took at the coroner's office, revealing the gruesome nature of the teenagers' deaths.

"Oh, my ..." Guy's voice trailed off. "I've never seen anything like that."

"If Walker laced some of the Cloverdale crystal meth with some chemical, those deaths weren't accidental," Kelly said.

"Those are some serious allegations, Kelly," Guy chimed, fully engaged with his editor eye on the situation. "If you're going to make those charges, you need solid proof. But before that, you need to ask why he would do that in the first place."

"Good question. I'll let Cal answer that one," Kelly said, sensing Guy's sudden interest in telling this story. "In the meantime, we need to figure out what Walker was putting in the drugs at Cloverdale. We need to stop any more of those tainted drugs from getting in the distribution network, as crazy as that might sound."

"We can't do anything about today's shipment, but maybe we can stop tomorrow's if we alert the right people," Cal said.

"I've got a contact in forensics at the FBI field office in Salt Lake City. He owes me a favor. If you hustle, you can make it there in about two hours. I'll text you with details about where to meet him. And I'll stay here and figure out why Buddy Walker would be tainting drugs at Cloverdale."

"Sounds like a good plan, boss."

They all headed toward the exit, anxious to do some more digging, nervous about the off chance that Dawkins might wander into the barn at any moment.

"Oh, and Cal, take my Yamaha VMAX," Guy said, tossing him the key. "It's parked on the road that runs along the side of this property. That bike is a lot less conspicuous than Kelly's red sports car."

Dusk was beginning to settle in over southeastern Idaho. A long night lay ahead for *The Register*'s three most dedicated newsroom staff, who were unaware that this would be their final night as employees of the paper.

CHAPTER 48

WORD HAD NOT YET reached the security gate entrance to Cloverdale Industries when Walker rolled to a stop in front of the access arm.

He rolled down his window. Zack McDonald, the night shift guard, stood just outside his hut and hunched down to start an unwelcome conversation.

"Hi, Buddy," came McDonald's cordial greeting. "I heard you went home sick earlier today. You make a sudden recovery?"

Walker shifted in his seat, fingering the gun just out of sight from McDonald's view. He never knew McDonald to be rude, but he wasn't someone that could be easily fooled either. Shooting him would definitely gain him immediate access to the facility, but a mounting body count wouldn't help his already shaky cause. He took a deep breath and decided to keep lying.

"I'll be honest with you, McDonald, too much of Ray-Ray's barbecue isn't always a good thing, if you know what I mean. I feel OK now. Got no sick time either. If I don't get paid, I can't take care of my sick mother this month."

McDonald bought every lie. He raised the arm for Walker.

"Well, I hope you get to feeling a hundred percent soon. And the way you care for your mother, Walker ... You're an inspiration to us all."

Walker nodded and smiled. He let off the brake and eased on the gas. He heard Mercer snicker from the back seat, hidden beneath a blanket on the floorboard, just like Cal and Kelly had been a few hours earlier. Walker made it seem like that idea was hatched on the fly. But it was a protocol he had developed for Mercer when he needed to gain access to the facility.

Being in deep cover for five years in Statenville had taken its toll on Walker. He was itching to get out and get on with his life. Pretending to be a basketball coach and a part-time janitor was getting old, even if it meant bringing down what was long suspected to be one of the biggest drug cartels in the Pacific Northwest.

Before Walker had established enough evidence to put away the ringleaders for a long time, he needed to find out just how far the Cloverdale cartel extended. Who were the key players? How big of a sweep needed to be in place to bring down a supplier that seemed to proliferate the region? The lingering questions gnawed at Walker.

It was his impatience that caused his latest misstep, one that might cost him his job, especially if he didn't eliminate all the evidence. And in a town that was desperate to keep its dark secret hidden, its residents just might do the dirty work for him.

He parked his car near the back entrance to the plant and grabbed his backpack. In an effort to be cautious, Walker always parked in the only three parking spaces that weren't covered by security cameras. After a quick glance around the parking lot to make sure no one saw him, he tapped on the window and Mercer crawled out, still dressed in his deputy uniform.

Due to the earlier commotion at the plant, Walker missed his opportunity to set up his final domino before setting into motion a plan that would connect all the pieces of the twisted puzzle known as Cloverdale Industries and Statenville. But there was always another shipment going out. Always.

CHAPTER 49

AS DUSK FADED INTO night, the warm air turned cool and crisp. Riding two hours on a motorcycle through the Idaho and Utah mountains would be much more enjoyable during the day, but Cal didn't mind. Riding tandem with Kelly would make up for being unable to see most of the spectacular scenery.

It should have been a two-hour ride, but Cal trimmed 20 minutes off the trip by holding his speed steady at 10 miles an hour above the speed limit. The bright, burgeoning moon lit up the valley floor and illuminated the craggy mountain peaks. Making the trip in a convertible would've been better, Cal thought. At least he would've been able to talk with Kelly, maybe about something other than the most exciting day of their lives that was far from over. But then again, she probably wouldn't have hugged him for over an hour and a half straight.

Cal pulled into the empty parking lot and waited. Guy's instructions were to wait on a park bench on the backside of the pond at Sugar House Park. They were to make the drop by leaving the chemical samples they found with a flash drive of Kelly's pictures of the chemical equations in a paper bag. Cal found a couple of rocks by the water's edge and put them in the bag, weighing it down.

They sat on the bench and waited for their contact.

Kelly broke the silence.

"You know what's strange about this whole story?"

"What *isn't* strange about it?" Cal countered.

"No, there's definitely one thing that stands out to me as strange."

"What is it?"

"Well, I've lived in Statenville my whole life, and it is a tight-knit community. But when these kids died, it's like nobody cared. I just don't understand that."

"Maybe it's because it's part of Statenville's dirty little secret. Everybody seems to be hiding something."

"That's small town America, Cal. Everybody has their secrets, even the big city folks. But it's just more evident when you live in a small area and know everyone."

"Maybe. But this goes beyond something like the mayor having an affair with his secretary. This is something that somebody is willing to kill us over—and it feels like everybody. I just think—"

Cal abruptly ended his thought. A man wearing sweatpants and a windbreaker was approaching the bench.

They both got up so they wouldn't arouse suspicion, vacating the bench.

Cal and Kelly headed for the path that circled the lake. Cal looked back casually to see if the man was still there. He wasn't. Neither was the bag. The drop had been successful.

They walked back toward the parking lot and climbed on Guy's bike. The night was still young.

CHAPTER 50

MERCER KNEW WALKER'S TIME was short. A manhunt in Statenville didn't just include the small local law enforcement staff. It included all the thugs on Cloverdale's payroll, the ones so secret that not even Walker had figured out who they were. If Mercer was going to make his mark in the bureau, it was going to be helping Walker make a big move—and this was their big moment.

Mercer gave a misleading tip that sent Walker's search party clear across the county, far from Cloverdale Industries. In a short time, Mercer familiarized himself with the inner workings of the Statenville Sheriff's Department, including the protocol for a major security breach. The other deputies spoke in vague generalities until they felt they could trust Mercer. Once he passed a specifically designed trust test, Mercer became privy to more of Statenville's secrets. Then, he learned about the biggest secret of all.

But he and Walker were determined to expose it. Statenville and its mob-like leaders would no longer be the kingpin drug dealers of the Pacific Northwest. No, that was all about to stop.

Walker and Mercer both crouched low as they crept up the ramp toward the backside of the facility. One of Walker's first tasks was to discover the range of the security cameras and all their blind spots. And in this moment, that intel came in handy. Nobody saw them.

Mercer huddled close to a back-door entrance as Walker dug out his keys. Walker finally found the right one and opened the door. He flipped the light switch and dropped his keys. They landed on the cement floor, clanking out an eerie echo. Walker bent down to pick up the keys and froze. He and Mercer both scanned the warehouse. It was bare. Not so much as a forklift remained. Every shelving unit, every box, every packing table—gone.

Neither could hide the shock on their faces.

"Aaahhhhh!" Walker let out a scream. His plan was disintegrating. At this point, he didn't care who heard him, though from the looks of the now-cavernous warehouse it didn't appear that anyone was there.

"Tonight was the night!"

Mercer and Walker both slumped onto the floor. Years of work had vanished. If there was no FBI raid, there was no way to get all the evidence necessary to shut down Cloverdale. It was over. The upper brass would likely yank their field status. Back to being analysts and pushing paper after this failed operation. But at least they wouldn't have to live in Statenville—not everything was bad about this.

Mercer was undeterred.

"Look, let's split up. You look around here and see if you can find any places that could easily house such a transformation and I'll check out the other end of the plant. Let's meet back here in 15."

"OK."

Mercer walked stealthily against the wall for about 200 yards and disappeared into an unlit portion of the warehouse.

Meanwhile, Walker began making a sweep of the staging area, fretting that it was all in vain.

Suddenly the back door swung open and the sounds of feet running thundered from across the warehouse. Walker scrambled to face the noise. More than a dozen high-powered rifles were pointed at them from a handful of directions.

Walker surrendered immediately.

"Hey, don't shoot. I'll do whatever you want us to do," he

pleaded.

Not a single person moved, frozen with the pair in their sights.

"Seriously, guys. I'm sure we can work something out."

Mayor Gold, who had been standing off to the side against the wall, stepped forward.

"I'm sure we can," Gold said.

"Mayor Gold? What are you doing here?"

"Maybe I should ask you the very same question since you obviously don't know anything about basketball or cleaning a facility."

"And you don't know anything about keeping a secret."

"Oh, I beg to differ special agent Walker. I can call you 'special agent,' can't I?"

"I've got plenty of footage and pictures of what really goes on here."

"Really? So, special agent Walker, tell me what really goes on here."

"I think we all know."

"What? That this facility produces faulty healthcare and vitamin products for mass consumption? Everyone already knows that."

"No, I mean that this company uses its vast distribution network and resources to transport drugs."

"Well, I wouldn't call them drugs. They're more like vitamins."

Gold smiled at his wry comeback.

"No, I mean illegal drugs," Walker said, trying to remain serious.

"Drugs? Here?" Gold gestured with his hand toward the barren warehouse.

"You know you're never going to get out of this without the FBI taking this town apart. They will find something."

"Perhaps they'll find your dead body ... right next to agent Cooper's."

The comment by normally affable Gold chilled Walker. He had hoped up until now it was merely bravado talk. It wasn't. Nobody knew about agent Cooper. Even within the FBI he was a ghost— not to mention a well-respected legend. But Walker didn't have time for respect when Cooper came into town unannounced.

Cooper wanted to glean enough information to make an assessment as to whether the undercover operation was going as planned—or if it was even necessary. Plus there were rumors within the bureau that Walker was breaking protocol. Cooper was there on assignment—and the assignment was Walker. But apparently Gold's goons had ended that assignment.

With a slight motion toward Walker, the armed men surrounding him moved in. They snatched Walker's hands behind his back and secured his wrists with plastic zip ties.

* * *

Operation Fuego had been jettisoned for *Operation Cleanup.* Gold gambled that the FBI agents wouldn't have sent any hard evidence back to their superiors—or even if they had it would be inadmissible as evidence in court.

Gold hoped this day would never come, but knew exactly what to do in case it did. Agent Cooper's presence was a surprise, as was Mercer's. Gold thought there was only one man on the case—and that was Walker. But Gold had a contingency plan or five. When you've got a secret as deep as the one Statenville held, there was no need to take any chances.

And Gold wouldn't take a single chance with Walker and Mercer. After securing the FBI pair, Gold's men forced the two to take a hit of meth. It had all been well thought out by Gold; planting evidence on the two men would completely undermine any federal case against Cloverdale Industries. A drugged out janitor? A coach who others would testify gave drugs to students, including the ones who died? Who would find him credible, even if he was believed to be an FBI agent?

Gold returned to the confines of his home and had been there 30 minutes when his cell phone rang.

"Gold, here."

"Mr. Gold, the threat has been eliminated," came the voice on the other end, emotionless.

"Excellent. Keep me posted on how that other loose end is coming along."

Gold hung up the phone and smiled. It had been a while since he had smiled. A long time ago, Gold learned that suppressing grief was never good—not even for a few days. But it had served him well during this process.

It was almost safe to cry.

***

The man climbed into his F-250 truck and roared away, leaving carnage in his wake.

Walker's body now laid slumped over the steering wheel, still clutching his firearm. Dead. Two close-range bullet holes to the head. No law enforcement personnel would report that his body had been moved and his body repositioned.

Outside Mercer's car was old man Willie Nelson, lying face down in the gravel next to the road. He had been groomed for such a moment as this: the perfect junkie on which to pin a murder. He held the murder weapon in his hand. One bullet to the head. One to the chest. A small plastic baggie of meth in his pocket.

Gold's men had successfully recreated the scene that Gold had envisioned when he drew up this plan. One dead junkie. One dead basketball coach. A drug deal gone bad. Walker? An FBI agent? Nobody would believe that, except maybe the players on his basketball team who knew he had no idea how to coach the sport. He worked two jobs just to support his illicit lifestyle, not his mother who had actually died five years ago. Gold had enough details of Walker's life that he could paint him however he wanted and no one would question him. Perception is always more powerful than reality when you control the information. A drug dealer was more like it—a dealer trying to sell meth to a known crazy person in Willie Nelson. The whole town knew he was nuts.

Framing people was an art form—and the people of Statenville had been painting Louvre-worthy canvases for snooping parties for 20 years. If anyone managed to make it out alive, the person's reputation was sullied beyond repair, and their word was rendered meaningless.

Cal and Kelly were next.

CHAPTER 51

LIKE THE WHEELS ON the Vmax, Cal's mind couldn't stop spinning. He was creating scenarios in his head of what was really happening at Cloverdale Industries—some good, some bad. But he couldn't logically believe he saw something he shouldn't have. People were dead. Drugs were visible. His life was in danger. What other physical evidence could trump the empirical evidence he already had? What Cal had might not stand up in a court of law, but it already won a gavel-banging judgment in the court of his own opinion. The one thing that ate at him was Walker's connection to the situation. What was he doing there? And why did he tie them up?

Cal allowed Kelly's embrace from the rear seat on the motorcycle to interrupt his furious theory building. In the midst of running for their lives, Cal's fondness for Kelly was pushed to the edge of his consciousness. This wasn't some action movie. The two stars of this adventure didn't have time to share a passionate kiss before he ran at the bad guys with guns blazing while she admired her man's bravery. No, this wasn't Hollywood. There was no dramatic music, no feeling that everything would eventually be fine. But, oh how Cal wished it was. Having Kelly nestled up to him was heaven enough considering the circumstances.

Buzzzzzz. Buzzzzz.

Cal's phone jolted him back to reality. He slowed down the bike and pulled over. There were only two people he was interested in talking to: Guy and somebody from the FBI field office in Salt Lake City. The "restricted" name listed on his iPhone's caller ID let him know it was the latter.

Cal walked away from the bike with Kelly. They took a few steps toward an open range with scattered cattle roaming about for an evening snack. He answered the phone.

"Hello?"

"Cal?"

"Yes."

"This is Eric from the FBI's Salt Lake City field office."

"Hi, Eric. Did you find out anything?"

"Well, this isn't normal protocol, but this isn't a normal situation. You need to do everything in your power to keep this substance from getting into the public's hands."

Cal said nothing.

"It appears that the chemical agent being manufactured is CPZ—and in high doses."

"How dangerous is CPZ? What does it do?"

"In small quantities, not much. It's used to treat psychosis patients. But in large quantities, it can do a lot of things."

"Like what?"

"Like shut your liver down for one thing—and shut it down in a hurry, especially when it's combined with other accelerants."

"What accelerants?"

"Methamphetamine would cause it to start working quickly."

Cal's heart was pounding. All those questions that nagged him since he started investigating were now beginning to have plausible answers.

"And what kind of symptoms would manifest as a result of the liver shutting down?"

"There are plenty of things that happen. For one, the person would look jaundiced. But the most painful that would present, physically, is all the bile seeping into the blood stream."

"What would that do?"

"It would create an intense itching sensation all throughout a person's body, much like suffering from the autoimmune disease, Primary Sclerosing Cholangitis. Due to liver malfunction, PSC causes itching beneath the surface of the skin and renders scratching that area useless. You can scratch all you want, but the itching sensation never goes away. That bile is still there, underneath the skin, irritating you."

"So, if you put this high dosage of CPZ with an accelerant, how would it impact someone?"

"Well, it's not deadly in and of itself, but the itching would be intense."

"Intense enough that you could scratch yourself to death?"

"I suppose that's possible, but I've never heard of such a thing. I don't know how any lab would sign off on the testing of this chemical on animals for the express purpose of shutting down the liver—so I doubt that's a question we could ever answer."

Cal had sufficient information at this point to draw some obvious conclusions, but he never ceased to marvel at how last-second questions seemed to produce the juiciest pieces of information.

"Any other information I should be aware of?"

"Well, in doing some cursory research, I found that the FBI once had a team of people working on a way to use CPZ as markers in drugs, much like what you mentioned with methamphetamines. They wanted to figure out a way to mark drug users and substantial dealers' distribution networks. The strange nature of the cases would send out an alert to the CDC from which the FBI could obtain basic information on the spread of a dealer's network."

"So what happened to the program?"

"In 2008, they tried it in field tests by undercover operatives in three cities—Seattle, L.A., and Phoenix—by tainting an individual dosage—and each time the drug user died, though the report I read didn't say from what. So, they disbanded the program. That's not the kind of publicity the FBI wants, even if it helps accomplish its end game."

"End game of what? Eliminating drug pushers?"

Eric answered with nervous laughter then continued.

"Well, interestingly enough, both Walker and Mercer were part of those teams that did the testing."

Cal knew he wasn't getting another answer out of him.

"Thanks for your help, Eric."

"No problem, Cal. I'll let my superiors know and hopefully we'll have someone in Statenville tomorrow to investigate what's going on. I'm sure we'll find you."

Cal hung up the phone. The last thing he wanted was anybody finding him, especially the FBI. His list of theories was growing—and Kelly looked anxious to hear what he had learned.

Five minutes into rehashing his phone conversation and introducing a new theory, Cal's iPhone buzzed again—this time, it was Guy.

"Where are you guys, Cal?"

"We're about 30 minutes outside of Statenville. Why?"

"Don't come back. Head back to Salt Lake or somewhere nearby. Things are getting ugly here, and I know you're next. If they find out I helped you, they'll kill me."

"Whoa. Slow down, Guy."

"No, I'm serious—especially if they see you on my bike. That's bad news for both of us. There'll be no doubt then who helped you."

"So, what am I supposed to do? Stay in Salt Lake City? And for how long? I'm almost broke. I work at *The Register*, remember?"

"OK, call the paper and ask for Dave Youngman. Tell him that you're a friend of mine and that I asked him to take you in as a favor."

"Then what?"

"Then, you write your story. Does Kelly have her camera?"

"Yep, she's got it."

"OK, put together her best photos with your story and send it to *The Tribune* in Salt Lake and *The Times* in Seattle. I'll let those editors know your story is coming."

"And they'll print it, Guy?"

"If I tell them you're trustworthy, they will. They'll know what to do with it."

"OK. Thanks, Guy. Take care."

"You, too."

It had always been Cal's dream to write for *The Times*. He never believed he would be writing about a mind-bending conspiracy with the hard evidence in hand to prove its truth. Nor did he think he would get a 1A byline story before his friend, Josh.

But then, neither did he ever imagine anyone would hunt him down with the express purpose of killing him.

CHAPTER 52

THERE WERE ONLY TWO reasons Mayor Gold ever drank alcohol. The first was to celebrate on New Year's Eve. The second was when pacing wouldn't calm his nerves. New Year's Eve assured that the bottle of Crown Royal hidden in his study would never go a year without taking a hit. However, uncapping his secret elixir rarely occurred before the annual visit from his in-laws at Thanksgiving. This year, he was three months ahead of schedule.

Pacing and drinking only hyped up Gold. He preferred to take his whisky sitting down. But he didn't know if anything could settle him at this hour. Presiding over the murder of not one but two FBI agents was enough to make him consider searching for a barrel of whisky. But he knew that would be the least of his problems if the feds discovered what exactly Statenville was up to. All he could now was wait.

The clock ticked slowly. It was 10:30 p.m. Thus far, Gold's contingency plan had been executed flawlessly. However, the two reporters trying to be superheroes threatened to mar his precious ointment. For years, Gold held *The Register* under his thumb, buying off editors with the publisher firmly in his pocket. He never really considered a reporter from *The Register* having the ability to flesh out this story, much less two of them. They usually consisted of halfwits who – if they somehow graduated from community college – struggled to write a well-constructed sentence. But the economy's poor state flooded the market with able-bodied reporters, even *The Register* had jobs available that appealed to top journalism students. They had to write somewhere. Gold had underestimated Cal's skills and wherewithal to pursue this story. It was a rare mistake.

Gold looked at his watch again and took another pull on his whisky. He figured Yukon Grant was about 30 minutes away from correcting that mistake.

Keeping a secret of this magnitude requires a commitment to sacrificing profit to keep it silent. When you tell people you're going to pay them, you pay them. And when they do a great job, you sometimes pay them more than you agreed. Happy employees don't blow whistles. Keeping a secret like this also requires the guts to do the dirty work. This was the part that Gold didn't like, but one he accepted as a necessary evil.

He didn't simply dislike the dirty work—he loathed it. But Yukon wasn't the only one with an assignment. There was one job Gold needed to finish on his own. He drained the last drop of whisky and grabbed his 9 millimeter handgun. His work was almost done.

***

Guy hung up the phone. He wasn't sure if he could convince his old paper, *The Tribune*, to run Cal's story, but he had pulled it off. He had done the same with *The Times*, too. If Cal could put together what Guy thought he was capable of, tomorrow might bring relief. No more lies. No more deception.

He began buttoning up the house for the evening, shuffling from room to room in his robe, turning off all the lights and securing all the doors and windows. His bedtime routine consisted of being fully ready for bed and sitting up for his DVR replay of the late local news. It was a luxury never afforded to him so early in the evening while working the late shift at a daily newspaper. But working at a weekly newspaper with 9 to 5 hours almost every day made him feel like he had a somewhat normal life. At least now he could slice up his time into convenient and predictable parcels like most Americans.

Guy had just finished brushing his teeth when he froze.

Tap. Tap. Tap.

Somebody was knocking at his backdoor.

Guy crept back toward the kitchen, unsure of who might be dropping by unannounced at this late hour. Would it be Cal and Kelly ignoring his warning to stay out of Statenville? Would it be one of the mayor's thugs?

He grabbed a wooden baseball bat from the large floor vase he used to store his umbrella—and other objects handy during a home invasion. He inched closer to the door and flipped the back door light on.

It was Mayor Gold.

Guy exhaled. He slid the baseball bat back into the vase and swung the door open.

"Mayor Gold. What brings you out here at this time of night?"

"We need to talk," Gold said. "May I come in?"

"Sure. What's going on?"

This wasn't Gold's first time visiting Guy. Gold strode through the kitchen and into the den, while Guy scrambled to turn on some lights. They sat on opposing couches with only a glass coffee table separating them.

"I know it's late, so I'll be brief," Gold started.

"So, what's going on?"

"Well, I need to ask you a very important question."

"OK, shoot."

"Why did you help Cal and Kelly escape Statenville today? I was under the impression that you had been instructed to keep them pre-occupied with other assignments so they wouldn't be digging too deep on things that are best left alone."

"What do you mean? I didn't help them do anything but their job."

"Well, I know your VMAX is missing and we've had reports from several people that Cal and Kelly were seen on it heading out of town. Care to explain?"

"I don't know what you're talking about."

"Should we go to your garage and look at your VMAX."

"I don't think that's necessary. You know I would never break our agreement."

Gold didn't say a word. He pulled a digital recorder out of his pocket and placed it on the coffee table. He pushed play.

"... *put together her best photos with your story and send it to* The Tribune *in Salt Lake and* The Times *in Seattle. I'll let those editors know your story is coming.*

"*And they would print it, Guy?*"

"*If I tell them you're trustworthy, they will. They'll know what to do with it.*"

Gold pushed stop.

"Would you care to revisit your last statement, Guy?"

Guy avoided eye contact and said nothing.

"I thought you were on our side, Guy. I really did. I trusted you. But that is unforgivable."

Guy knew he should've known better. Tapping his phone should have been a given, especially with the suspicious treatment he received earlier in the day. But he was careless.

Gold pulled out his gun and pointed it at Guy.

"You'll never get away with this, you know? I know deep down you're a decent man. You wanted to make a better life for people in this town, but you made some poor choices a long time ago. You don't have to take another innocent life."

"You're not innocent, Guy—stand up!"

Gold was already standing, while Guy slowly rose from the couch, placing both hands in the air as to surrender. However, Guy knew this wasn't a time to surrender. In a matter of minutes, Gold was going to fill him with lead, dump his body and have a tight alibi and plausible story about Guy's accidental death.

"Go get some jeans and a shirt on. We're going outside. Move it!"

Guy had resigned himself that this was the end. With all the accidental deaths in Statenville, you would've thought local clothing shops only offered shoes in pairs of left feet. Guy knew the truth behind every single one, but printed the invented version fed to him by local law enforcement. He knew his story would be no different.

Well, if I'm going to die, I'm not going to make it easy on the mayor.

Gold marched behind Guy as he moved through the kitchen toward his bedroom. Just as Guy was about to leave the kitchen, he lunged for his baseball bat.

Gold didn't even wait for Guy to turn around. He shot Guy twice in the back and once in the head.

Guy fell toward the corner, his head slamming against the now blood-spattered wall. He slumped face-first to the ground, his maroon robe turning a deeper hue of red.

* * *

Gold looked at the mess in Guy's kitchen. One of his workers would scour the house. It would be spotless when Sheriff Jones came to do a standard investigation on the strange death of Guy Thompson, who would drown in a fishing accident on the Snake River. A number of witnesses would see him fishing that evening after work. But only the coroner would see his body, falsifying his report about the cause of death. A cremation would follow since the next of kin never responded.

Gold sighed and looked at his watch. He couldn't stand waiting much longer to hear from Yukon. If Gold was lucky, Cal and Kelly would be in Yukon's possession right now.

CHAPTER 53

CAL AND KELLY NEEDED to find a makeshift workstation and fast. The nearest possibility was about 20 miles back in the town of Ellington, which had a McDonald's. Covering the Statenville-Ellington football game the year before, Cal learned that the dining room in the Ellington McDonald's stayed open until midnight on the weeknights and 2 a.m. on the weekends. It was the only eating establishment open late at night in Ellington with the exception of Esther's Café and Eats located inside a local gas station.

When they pulled into the McDonald's parking lot fifteen minutes later, it was nearly vacant. Cal hated writing in public places, but if it was quiet at least he could begin to organize his thoughts and pound out a story. Between the two of them, they had three pieces of equipment: two iPhones and a camera.

"You start uploading photos and video to a drop box somewhere and I'll start writing."

Cal wasted no time and began pecking away. Kelly hooked up her SD card reader to her iPhone and went to work, uploading videos and photos that backed up the extraordinary claims they were about to make.

Most of Cal's story was written in his head so it didn't take him long to turn it into a thrilling read in an email to be sent off to two major metro dailies.

* * *

Yukon rolled down his window and adjusted the mirror on his black F-250. After all the excitement this evening had wrought, he wasn't too worried about anyone following him. The blood stains on his hands gave him all the reassurance he needed. Statenville's hallowed secret was dangerously close to being exposed. But there was only one more obstacle to make it safe again.

He scanned every approaching set of headlights, searching for a single one, a motorcycle's.

They've got to be out here somewhere.

Yukon understood just how high the stakes were if Cal and Kelly eluded his grasp and broadcast a fanciful story. It was a story that would struggle to be supported given the carnage left in Yukon's wake. Some secrets are best left unuttered, even if the people trying to expose them do so with a custom-fitted tin foil hat. There always seemed to be some shred of truth in what conspiracy theorists claimed. In Statenville's case, a shred could be damaging. Yukon had already been to jail after resorting to crime to make ends meet. Not even a GED was enough to earn him a job as a mechanic in Statenville. But that was before his acquired prison skills became vital for Mayor Gold. Life was good now. And he wasn't going back – not to a life of petty theft and certainly not to prison.

His hair whipped in the cool evening air. Yukon stroked his scraggly beard and smiled, plotting all the ways he would rage on Cal and Kelly before killing them and depositing their bodies in Cold River Canyon, his favorite dumping ground. This time, he wouldn't fail to finish the job.

So far, the long stretch of highway from Statenville to Salt Lake City had been quiet, mostly semi trucks transporting their wares from one Western outpost to another. An occasional car interrupted the monotony with the flicker of bright to dim headlights, but not a single motorcycle on the road.

Up ahead, a city limits sign reflected his headlights. He began slowing down. He didn't want to attract any more attention than necessary at this time of night.

Yukon had arrived in Ellington.

* * *

"Pick up the phone, Guy!" Cal said. "Why aren't you answering?"

Kelly finished uploading the last of her photos and videos to her personal storage server in cyberspace. She then decided to answer Cal's rhetorical question.

"Maybe he's on the run again."

"From who? For all they know, Guy is one of *them*, remember?"

"What if they found out he wasn't?"

"They wouldn't try anything on Guy. He's too prominent of a figure in the community."

"That's an assumption I'm not willing to make so quickly, Cal. I think we're barely scratching the surface on the depths to which this town will go to hide its dark secret."

"Well, if they killed him, they would have to kill us, too."

"That's what I'm afraid of. Somebody has already tried it once today. Maybe two groups of people for all we know."

"With all the evidence that we have, there's no stopping this thing now. Statenville will be flush with the 21st Century's version of a gold rush – a national media frenzy on a compelling story that includes a government conspiracy."

"If we have enough proof."

"What do you mean, Kelly? We've got all the proof we need. A coroner's report. Our own investigative videos. Corroborating testimony. Not to mention people who would all sing to avoid a harsh prison sentence."

"I know, but as good as it sounds to us, those editors have to be willing to stick their necks out for us. And what if they're not? And what if we wake up tomorrow and all the witnesses are dead?"

"Look who sounds like the conspiracy theorist now?"

"I'm just saying that we still need to be careful, Cal. Just because we have evidence doesn't mean anyone is going to believe us."

"Don't worry. After I talk to Guy and send this story in, nobody will touch us. Doing so would only implicate them more."

"I hope you're right – just hurry up, OK?"

A familiar engine roar filled the north parking lot. Cal froze. He knew where he had heard it before – the night his car had gone careening off the road. He cut his eyes toward the window and saw a long-haired muscular man climbing out of his Ford F-250. Getting instructions from Guy would have to wait.

"Kelly, grab your stuff and follow me right now," Cal said in a low calm voice.

"Why, Cal?"

"Just do it," he barked in a whisper.

Cal slipped his iPhone in his pocket. Kelly crammed her camera back into her backpack and they exited on the south side of the restaurant and headed for the Vmax.

He turned back to locate the man – and he was gone.

"Hurry, Kelly. We've got to leave now!"

CHAPTER 54

"THWACK!"

Cal was just about to put on his helmet when a forearm shiver knocked him to the ground. Disoriented and lying face down on the pavement, Cal began looking for Kelly.

"Run, Kelly! Run!"

Had Cal been more aware, he would've seen that his instructions were meaningless. Kelly's legs dangled off the ground as Yukon wrapped his meaty arms around her body that suddenly seemed frail. She shrieked and struggled. Her actions were futile – and she knew it.

Yukon cast an ominous shadow over Cal.

"Get up, kid. ... You ever heard of a *dead*line?"

Cal rolled over to see the long-haired man clutching Kelly in one hand and a crowbar in the other. Groggy from the blow, Cal moved slowly. It wasn't fast enough for Yukon.

"Let's go now," Yukon bellowed as he snatched Cal into the air and began shoving him around the back of the restaurant to the other side of the parking lot. The truck was their destination.

Cal wanted to fight and be Kelly's hero, but he knew he didn't stand a chance.

Just be smart and stay alive. You'll think of something.

Yukon snatched Cal by the back of his collar and hoisted him a few feet off the ground before pushing him into the back of his pickup bed. Cal had almost fully recovered from the earlier blow, but decided to play the part of a wounded animal. He did as he was told.

"Don't go tryin' to be a hero, kid," said Yukon, who maintained his tight grip on Kelly. "You just might end up dead sooner rather than later."

Cal nodded and sat still, awaiting his next instruction.

Yukon then grabbed Kelly with both hands and lifted her into the pickup bed as well. He ripped her backpack off, confiscating the damning evidence. He took some rope out of his toolbox in the truck bed and began securing Kelly's feet together. He then pulled her hands by her side and ran the rope around her midsection a few times. The last touch was the gag, though by this time Kelly had stopped hurling insults. Cal got the same treatment.

***

Yukon covered the reporters with a tarp, securing it on all four corners with bungee cord. *This is better than the time I killed two elk in one day.* Yukon was reveling in the fact that he would get to keep his way of life after all.

Time to report the good news. Yukon called Gold.

"I got 'em," Yukon said before Gold could utter a word.

"And the evidence?"

"It's sitting next to me on the front seat. And those two aren't going anywhere, except on a quick trip to Cold River Canyon."

"Well done. Dump the bodies and bring me what evidence you confiscated."

"You got it, boss."

Yukon's F-250 began rumbling. Statenville justice had to be served.

***

Neither Cal nor Kelly made a sound for the first two minutes of their ride to an eventual murder scene. Cal glanced over at Kelly after he heard what sounded like a muffled sob. Tears were streaming down Kelly's face.

When Cal begged Kelly for help on this story a day earlier, he certainly didn't think that they would be bound, gagged, and headed for their deaths less than 48 hours later. But as a professional reporter whose business was dealing in facts, Cal had to recognize them. There was no cavalry coming. No one was going to save them. No one wanted to hear the truth – and they wouldn't. The truth was about to be buried with them.

Cal grew sick thinking that he was going to die next to the woman he now had feelings for.

But that wasn't a fact. Not yet, anyway. There was still time.

CHAPTER 55

MERCER SAT IN HIS parked car, a couple houses down and across the street from Guy's house. He wanted to talk to Guy and warn him that Gold was tying up all his loose ends – and Guy would be considered one of them. But it looked like he was too late. Gold's car was already parked outside when Mercer had arrived.

Finally, there was movement outside of Guy's house. The front porch light went dark. Then the outside flood light on the side of the house went dark. Mercer could make out Gold's shadowy figure sneaking out of the house and to his car.

As soon as Gold's car disappeared down the street, Mercer opened his car door and sprinted down the street to Guy's house. Careful not to leave any prints, Mercer smashed the windowpane closest to the door knob and reached through the remaining shards with a handkerchief to open the door from the inside.

As soon as Mercer stepped inside, he saw Guy's body with blood pooling around him. He checked for a pulse. Nothing. Gold had eliminated a possible whistle blower. There was little doubt in Mercer's mind that he would receive a call in less than ten minutes to take Gold's body and move it to another place, make it look like an accident. Mercer knew the drill far too well.

Acting quickly, Mercer put on a pair of latex gloves and began combing through Guy's personal effects.

He went straight for Guy's computer. No password lockout. Just an open window of Guy's home email inbox. Mercer saw a response from two email accounts, one ending in seattletimes.com and the other ending in sltrib.com. Guy had been communicating with other newspapers. Mercer opened the sent folder and read two emails to two editors who were acquaintances, informing them about an impending story that may come from a reporter named Cal Murphy. He stated a photographer named Kelly Mendoza would also send photos and other evidential material.

Then Mercer found Guy's cell phone on the kitchen table. Undoubtedly a few key entries had been deleted. The last call was to what appeared to be a local cell number about 45 minutes ago. According to the call records, the final one was a minute and a half long, much longer than the time it probably took for Gold to announce he was going to drop by and discuss a few things.

Mercer redialed the number.

***

Cal felt a familiar vibrating sensation in his pants pocket. He figured it was Guy calling with instructions on where to file his nonexistent story, a story that might never get written. The buzzing served as a reminder of his frustration, but it also reminded him of something else as it made an awkward clanging sound: It reminded him of his pocket knife.

Sure, it was small. Cal could've probably hid it in his mouth if he needed to. But in his haste to finish his assignment, Yukon didn't confiscate cell phones, making the assumption that everything he needed was in Kelly's bag. But then, it wasn't like he was figuring either of the bound reporters could make an escape. Not at 75 miles an hour. Not with arms and legs bound in the bed of a pickup truck. Not on his watch.

Cal's hope returned. He began scooting closer to Kelly. Cal was already working on a plan.

CHAPTER 56

COME ON! PICK UP *the phone, Cal!*

Mercer felt the walls crumbling around him. Everything he and Walker had uncovered to build their case against Mayor Gold and Cloverdale Industries was vanishing. With Walker and his reckless ways gone for good, Mercer knew how he wanted the story to be written. He was going to be the hero—and the FBI would be innocent. After all, they were just protecting the public, for the greater good.

But Mercer's ability to spin the story his way was slipping away. He had to know what Cal and Kelly knew. If he could only reach them.

* * *

As Yukon sped down the highway, Cal felt like the anxious driver was determined to jar every tooth loose in the remaining 30 minutes he had. It made Cal all the more determined. He began sawing through Kelly's ropes with the precision of a heart surgeon. Despite the ticking clock, Cal knew this was no time for shortcuts or sharp cuts to the flesh. He had to cut Kelly free so she could return the favor—and the job needed to be done right.

Despite the seconds feeling as if they were hours, Cal eventually sliced his way through Kelly's cords in about two minutes. She pulled the gag out of her mouth before pulling Cal's off.

"Spin around so I can cut your feet loose," Cal said to Kelly as he shouted above the whooshing wind and the flapping tarp.

Kelly didn't hesitate to follow orders. Despite the gag being removed, she didn't say a word. She was focused – and shaking.

Fifteen seconds later, Cal was ripping his way through the rope around Kelly's feet. Despite having his hands bound, Cal figured he could cut her loose more quickly – and if this ride abruptly ended, he figured at least one of them could escape to tell the story of what was happening in Statenville.

Cal preferred they escape together. Eluding danger brought an adrenaline rush, but the potential of going on an adventure with Kelly seemed to heighten Cal's excitement. This could be a high stakes game of hide and seek, but Cal liked his chances with Kelly facing the formidable – only in stature – Yukon.

Cal cut Kelly's feet bindings free in about 90 seconds. He was quickly picking up on how to operate a pocketknife in pressure situations with his hands tied together. He had never done it before. But it made no difference now. Kelly was free.

"Start with my feet first," Cal yelled to Kelly, who began cutting away on Cal's ropes.

Since Cal could only guess at where they were headed, if he was wrong he at least wanted to be able to make a run for it. Free hands and bound feet meant nothing but a few parting shots before Yukon would subdue him and carry Cal to his grave. Free feet? That at least gave him a chance.

Kelly had almost finished cutting his feet loose when the truck slammed 90 degrees to the right. Kelly slid to the right as did Cal, whose shoulder saved his head from a blow against the side of the truck bed. The constant hum of four-wheel mud-grip tires on the pavement switched to the crackling sound of dirt. Cal figured his speculation about where they were headed was right: Cold River Canyon.

Based on his best guess, Cal also calculated that Kelly had about five minutes to cut him totally free before entering the foothills. Once in the foothills, the never-ending maze of hills and valleys would make it a daunting challenge for the two of them to escape alive before an all-out search party hunted them down.

Kelly kept hacking away before she cut Cal's legs free from the rope. Then she got to work on his hands.

"Kelly, keep cutting but listen to me," Cal said. "We've got to make a run for it the minute this truck slows down. There's probably only one more place he's going to halfway slow down that gives us a chance to jump out and run for it, OK? So, just follow my lead."

Kelly nodded, too focused to even expend energy responding.

She, too, had quickly learned how to hasten the process while ensuring that the cut was clean. In two minute's time, she had cut Cal free.

Just as she had finished cutting him free, the truck slowed to a stop – but it was much earlier than Cal had anticipated. Cal's best guess was that the final turn onto Cold River Canyon Road was at least another three minutes away.

Where are we? And why are we stopping?

CHAPTER 57

WORRIED AND FRUSTRATED AT the lack of response from Cal, Mercer decided it was best to get back into his patrol car and not yield to the paranoia that was gnawing at Gold. The killing spree over the past 24 hours proved Gold's resolve to insulate the Cloverdale empire from any scurrilous accusations. If there was any doubt before about Gold's determination to protect what he had built, it was snuffed out with Guy's last breath. Nobody was going to penetrate Statenville's fortress. It was an outpost that fell off almost every radar, the exact reason Gold methodically picked this city for his business.

But Gold put it on the FBI's radar. When Mercer joined the bureau, his first assignment at the Boston field office was to look for ways to bring down the Scarelli mob bosses. Gold, who went by Carmen Deangelo on the street, was a rising captain with great promise before he almost vanished. For about 12 years, the FBI's best assumption was that Deangelo had been killed quietly and buried in a place he would never be found.

However, Deangelo resurrected himself as Gold hundreds of miles away in a town he was sure the FBI had never heard of. And he was right. Most people in the FBI's Salt Lake field office had no idea where Statenville was, even though it was just a short drive north. That's because it was a typical small agricultural community where the biggest crimes committed were drunk driving and the occasional construction of a meth lab. Yet, Gold made one mistake five years ago that extinguished his anonymity with the FBI: one tidy job tipped off the bureau.

When Deangelo was in Boston, his crime scene signature was a U.S. gold coin from the late 1800s stuffed into the mouth of his victim. The FBI had at least a dozen murder victims demarcated by these rare gold coins, but proving Gold actually committed the crimes was another issue. The fact that most of Gold's victims were members of a rival mob did nothing to encourage the FBI to pursue the futile investigations further. If Gold did their dirty work without all the messy trials, the FBI was satisfied – even if it was wrong.

But Deangelo's signature reappeared about 12 years after the last gold-mouth murder – but it wasn't in Boston. This victim was in Portland – and he wasn't the member of a rival mob. Call it a reflexive flashback. Deangelo later lamented leaving his signature, but he figured no one would make the link. The gumshoe cops in Portland might overlook a detail that would be rehashed and analyzed in Boston. Maybe Deangelo would get lucky. But he didn't.

The man he killed was the 19-year-old son of U.S. Senator Tom Brazenworth, just a kid who got mixed up with the wrong crowd. This wasn't a case that was going to get overlooked. When the FBI was called in to investigate, agents quickly recognized Gold's calling card and began searching for him, eventually discovering his new alias and tracing him back to the town of Statenville. Rumors swirled on the street in Seattle, Portland and Salt Lake that there was a small town in Idaho that had a drug plant, which could easily be considered a commercial production. It was replete with a fleet of vehicles to move the product around the Northwest virtually undetected.

Once the FBI confirmed Deangelo was now going by the alias of Gold, field agents were planted in Statenville under deep cover to gather prosecutable evidence on the operation and determine just how deep it went. Walker and Mercer were those two men, both with impeccable resumes and a past that could only be traced to the one created and vetted by the FBI. Both even had a couple of run-ins with the law on their background checks just so Gold wouldn't get suspicious. The plan was working flawlessly – until now.

Walker had grown impatient waiting for Gold to make a mistake. Over the past five years, Walker and Mercer had amassed a small library's worth of information on the location and movement of Gold's Cloverdale Industries. But the FBI did not embed the pair just to bust Gold – they wanted Gold and everybody that was with him. And that included people selling and moving Cloverdale's drugs on the streets and across state lines. The FBI wanted an epic headline—and Walker was going to give it to them.

But when Walker began tinkering with chemical formulas to tag drugs, Mercer urged him to look elsewhere for ideas. But Walker was undaunted and eventually Mercer relented. The FBI had shut down this particular research program for good reason – all the animals that were undergoing testing were dying horrific and painful deaths. Monkeys were almost ripping themselves apart and dying. Dogs scratched and clawed themselves to death. Officials determined it was a good idea in theory but one that lacked the ethical standard to be tested on humans.

Walker thought he knew better. His minor in chemistry gave him just enough knowledge to be dangerous – and to test the boundaries of what well-trained professional chemists within the bureau had determined was impossible. At first when Walker coerced Mercer to start inserting his chemicals into the drug batches, it was impossible to track the distribution locations of the drugs. Walker wasn't using enough to track an entire shipment. He needed to wreak enough havoc to ensure that it would show up on the CDC's radar. But it was impossible to control his portion, the small batch he had inserted into a shipment.

That's when he had the idea to mix the marker chemical into a batch of drugs he found in Riley Gold's car. The coaching staff knew there were a few players on the team who had recently started doing drugs, so Riley was an easy target. Walker thought he and Mercer would be able to observe Riley and any other teammates dumb enough to try the drug. But Walker never considered the fact that his chemical compound might kill people, despite Mercer's rational warnings. Now, Mercer was the remaining harbinger of convicting information regarding Gold – as well as the only person still alive who played a part in the death of Gold's son.

Walker had done Mercer no favors with his rush to make a splash for the bureau, but for now, Mercer was safe. He was careful to separate himself from Walker, both in the ever-watchful public eye of Statenville and with the bureau. Mercer needed to talk with Cal. Mercer needed to make sure the right story was going to come out in the news media, one that made him a hero, not a villain. Sure, he had participated in heinous acts, but he wasn't like Walker. Mercer was for good and he wanted Cal to write the story that way.

He called Cal again and this time left a voice mail:

"Cal, I'm really worried about you. We need to talk ASAP. Please don't report this story until I can get you what you need to make this story a blockbuster – a confession by Gold."

If the FBI wanted headlines, Mercer was going to give it to them. He wasn't about to let all his work in Statenville be in vain.

CHAPTER 58

CAL FROZE BENEATH THE tarp. Kelly did the same. Yukon had killed the engine. Still unsure of why they were stopped, Cal and Kelly's bewilderment ended when a train whistle ripped through the cool night air, piercing the silence. Cal knew exactly where they were.

"Kelly, when this truck starts moving, we're going to make a run for it," Cal whispered to Kelly, who appeared rather calm considering that they both might be just a few minutes away from a gruesome death. "You go over your side of the truck bed and I'll go over mine. I'm pretty sure I know where we are – and if I'm right, we are stopped between two cornfields. If we run in opposite directions as hard as we can, Yukon won't be able to catch us both."

"Then what?" Kelly asked.

"Find a ride to Salt Lake and meet me at *The Tribune* offices downtown. We'll figure out what to do next."

"Are you sure this will work?"

Cal lied. "Like a dream."

Kelly craned her neck toward Cal and gave him a kiss on the cheek. Though it was short, Cal was still stunned by the forward move from a woman who hadn't given any clear signals about her feelings for him.

"For good luck," Kelly whispered.

Cal knew it was more than that as he leaked a smile.

The final train car rumbled through the crossing and Yukon fired up his engine. As Cal and Kelly felt Yukon jamming the truck into gear and easing onto the gas, they both enacted Cal's plan, diving over the edge and sprinting into cornfields on opposite sides of the road. Neither looked back, but they could hear Yukon speeding away without a second thought. Within a minute, the summer air fell silent. Yukon was gone.

Cal knew he didn't have much time to find his way to a barn or silo to hide out until morning. Mayor Gold was likely to wake up the entire county and form an all-out search party for him and Kelly. But considering the distance they had covered and the fact that Yukon never checked on them, Cal felt like his chances of finding a safe haven were higher than Gold's men finding him first.

Nevertheless, Cal's speculation about what might happen once Yukon realized his truck bed was empty didn't assuage Cal's motivating factor at the moment: pure fear for his life. Two minutes after he had jumped out of the truck, Cal was still sprinting through the cornfield. Crisp leaves smacked him in the face, chest and legs as he churned through the soft Idaho soil. It was a simple task: one foot in front of the other as fast he could move it – then repeat. The faint sound of crickets chirping was drowned out by the furious noise of flesh slapping an endless parade of leaves. *Swish, swish, swish.* It was rhythmic. Yet it was a weak beat compared to Cal's heart, a heart pounding so hard that he just knew if he looked down at his chest he would've seen the outline of it pulsing through his shirt. But there was no time for that either.

Scanning the sky beyond the towering cornstalks, Cal noticed the faint outline of a barn. Now, he had a destination. Swish, swish, swish.

Twenty seconds later, Cal tore out of the field and slowed to catch his breath. He then crept toward the barn, hoping that no guard dogs would attack him. They didn't. The barn was a storage shed for hay, a standalone structure that separated the cornfield from a pasture. Hay bails were stacked to the rafters. The place was perfect.

Cal exhaled. He had made it – for now. Yukon wouldn't find him here. Not tonight anyway.

As Cal began building a small fortress out of the bails as a precautionary measure, he wondered about Kelly. Did she make it too? Is she as fortunate as me? Then he hoped for the best and pondered whether Kelly's kiss really was more than just a peck on the cheek. It felt like it to him, but maybe that's because he wanted it to be more. He spent a few more minutes thinking about it before shutting off his mind and going to sleep. His journey was far from over. With the powerful Mayor Gold unleashed, Cal knew danger was still crouching at the door.

CHAPTER 59

GOLD COULDN'T SLEEP. Refusing to show any emotion but anger despite his son's death, Gold's nerves became more frayed by the minute. And his anger grew. Tonight, he had already looked into the eyes of one man he considered his friend and killed him. Could he kill two more?

Gold decided he needed to oversee this final loose end himself. While he trusted Yukon with the darkest secrets Statenville and Cloverdale Industries held, he wanted to see the two reporters' dead bodies at the bottom of Cold River Canyon for himself. No more wondering what surprises would come his way the next day. This was going to end tonight.

Sitting in his car at the end of a dirt road in Cold River Canyon, Gold tapped his steering wheel as he awaited Yukon's arrival. He took another pull on the flask that he brought with him. Gold could be cold hearted, but even he needed help to get up the nerve to kill more than one person in a night. It wouldn't be the first time he had done this – but it had been a long time.

Gold slowly shook his head and closed his eyes, trying to ignore the nightmare scenario running through his mind that his empire would be busted. This wasn't what he wanted. He was tired of the killing, the dirty work that sucked away a portion of his soul with each person he murdered. It was why he left Boston. He couldn't escape a life of crime, but he could escape the murder. To Gold, selling drugs was a simple transaction, an exchange of cash for a product. What the buyers did with the drugs was up to them. He at least hoped they used and enjoyed it responsibly. But why anyone would want to do drugs was a mystery to Gold. Like any good businessman, he saw the need and created a way to supply product to meet the demand. Because dealing drugs was criminal, it required the extra level of difficulty that came naturally to Gold. For several years, he had masterminded the best crime scenario he could've ever imagined – filthy rich, no dirty work, and nobody poking their noses around his business.

But Cal and Kelly changed all that. They couldn't accept the coroner's report and leave well enough alone. Three teenagers overdosed on the same batch of drugs. Obviously the drugs were bad, which led to their deaths, right? No need to whip up some conspiracy out of thin air just to sell a few newspapers. The whole town consumed every word in every edition of the paper. This was never about selling newspapers.

Now Gold had to find his mayhem moxie and stamp out this substantial threat, Scarelli style. There wasn't going to be a trace left of them – not because Gold was vengeful; he learned a long time ago that vengeance got you nowhere. No, Gold disposed of dead bodies as a necessary precaution. He wasn't going to get pinned for someone's murder. He was likely to be a suspect or a "person of interest" should a full-blown murder investigation commence by outside law enforcement agencies. But Gold wouldn't be seriously implicated. He had slipped up five years ago by reverting back to his former self and inserting a gold coin into a victim's mouth. But he vowed not to do it again, ceasing to carry gold coins in his pocket so he could resist the temptation. He didn't want the FBI crawling all over his backyard. For Gold, a quiet crime was the best crime.

With his windows rolled down to take advantage of the cool summer breeze, Gold heard the sound of truck tires ripping down a dirt road. The glow of headlights illuminated the back of a boulder just off to the left of the road, announcing Yukon's impending arrival. The lights then beamed into Gold's car, getting larger as Yukon sped toward Gold. The truck skidded to a stop as a cloud of dust rushed by Gold.

Gold scrambled out of his car, anxious to put an end to his misery. The bodies of two dead reporters would do that for him.

* * *

Yukon climbed out of his truck and ambled toward the back of the bed where he met Gold.

"So, let's see them, Yukon," said Gold, dispensing with any formal greeting.

Yukon smiled and reached down to pull the tarp back but stopped himself cold. His smile morphed into a frown in a nanosecond, followed by a rant that included screaming and swearing. Four sacks of potatoes held down the bottom tarp; the top tarp layer was nowhere to be seen. Gold began seething.

"How could you let this happen, Yukon? Where did they escape?"

Yukon said nothing. He was busy retracing his steps, trying to think of where Cal and Kelly could've possibly escaped from his truck. A long and intense day of driving had likely left Yukon's timeline jumbled – well, that and the four beers he had chugged since capturing the pair. He couldn't come up with any theories – so he wisely offered none.

Yukon realized Gold had driven out to the canyon to see Cal and Kelly die firsthand. He knew his inability to keep his captives subdued let a once-manageable situation evolve into a more dangerous one – at least, dangerous in the sense that Cloverdale Industries could be exposed. Now they would be much more difficult to find.

Gold let out his anger on Yukon's truck, kicking the tires and slamming the side of the truck with his fist. He unleashed a few more rhetorical questions on Yukon, who stayed silent through the tirade. After a few minutes, Gold finished letting out his frustration with a final kick along the ground that sent pebbles flying through the air.

"Go find them, Yukon – and if you don't, don't bother coming back to Statenville."

Yukon knew Gold was serious. There was no more money to exchange hands, even if he was successful. So instead of launching a search that would have to extend multiple counties all the way to the Idaho border, Yukon decided to go home and pack his bags. If he was lucky, he might escape with his life. He would disappear. He was good at that, being a professional grifter, one who could undoubtedly find an employer in another town willing to pay for his services. Dead reporters or not, Yukon was through with Gold, Cloverdale Industries and Statenville. He knew he wouldn't miss it. There was no use being loyal to a man whose loyalty only extended as far as your usefulness to him.

CHAPTER 60

EVEN THE FIRST RAYS of sunshine weren't enough to wake Cal the next morning. Or the diesel engine of a John Deere 70 sputtering on the highway nearby. Or the barking dogs across the road. But he stirred when his iPhone buzzed, alerting him that he had a text message.

My phone!

In his rush to escape the night before, Cal had almost forgotten Yukon neglected to take his phone. He clamored to an upright position, brushing stray pieces of hay off of him before stretching. Waking up quickly wasn't a problem when adrenaline began coursing through his body again the moment he remembered why he slept in a barn as opposed to his bed. That and the lovely farm aroma wafting into the barn from the pasture just outside. Cal was wide awake.

He glanced down at the text message on his phone.

where r u?

Cal pounded back his answer in text script. He was east of the road where they had escaped, staying in a barn at the edge of the cornfield.

Cal waited a moment and then his phone buzzed again.

I'll b right there

Wondering how she would "be right there," Cal responded with a quick "awesome" and then began formulating a few plans to help them survive the day. And if they were lucky, maybe he and Kelly could write an article on the FBI's dirty little secret – and the truth behind Cloverdale Industries and Mayor Gold. It was difficult to see this idea becoming a reality in a timely manner, one that could happen before a deadline somewhere in the next 24 hours. But that thought remained secondary to survival – and surviving meant figuring out a way to leverage their knowledge of Cloverdale Industries and turning it into asylum. But Cal kept hitting mental dead ends. Maybe it was because he had yet to have his morning cup of coffee, something else that seemed unlikely given his current situation. Or maybe it was because Gold's stranglehold on the entire city of Statenville made it impossible to conceive of a plausible way to remove the bounty on his head. Either way, Cal was frustrated.

As promised, Cal looked up after about five minutes and saw a white delivery box truck bouncing along the farm road ruts toward the barn. A simple logo adorned both sides of the truck: Infinger Farms. The "i" in the middle of Infinger was a milk bottle with an apple over the top. Kelly had a big smile on her face, but the young farmhand driving the truck didn't share in her excitement.

The truck came to a stop just outside the barn, the engine still running. Cal approached the passenger side door where Kelly was climbing out.

"What in the world is this?" Cal asked, stunned at Kelly's resourcefulness. He had figured getting to Salt Lake would be an all-day affair. Could they really be going in a delivery truck?

"This is Infinger Farms' delivery truck – and this is T.J., who just so happens to be making a delivery of milk to an organic market in Salt Lake this morning."

"How did you find this?"

"Pure luck. I ran through the cornfield until I came to a clearing, which happened to be the edge of Infinger Farms' dairy complex. Mr. Infinger was checking on a sick cow when I came racing out of the field. At first he was cautious when I started telling him my story, then he eventually warmed up to me and realized I needed help. He took me to his house and let me stay in their guest room. And then this morning, after Mrs. Infinger cooked me a hearty country breakfast, Mr. Infinger offered to let us ride down to Salt Lake with T.J. So, here we are."

"What luck!"

"I even brought you a cup of coffee."

"You're an angel. Let's get moving. We've still got a lot to figure out."

Cal and Kelly climbed into the truck before Cal and T.J. formally introduced themselves to one another. Then they were on their way.

For the first 30 minutes of the drive, Cal and Kelly discussed strategies. They finally agreed upon a way they could gain leverage on Gold. The remaining two hours were spent talking about other fun outdoor adventures. None rivaled running for their lives the night before, but it was a nice diversion from the intensity of trying to survive a man – and town – bent on shoveling dirt on your grave as soon as possible.

At 11 a.m., the delivery truck rolled to a stop outside the steps of *The Tribune* offices.

"I think this is your stop," T.J. announced, anxious to get the giddy pair out of his truck.

After wishing him well, Cal and Kelly strode through the front doors and asked to see an editor. But not just any editor, *the* editor. The secretary met their request with disdain, shooting a "you guys know nothing about newspapers" glance at them. She dialed an extension anyway, confident they would be shooed away like pesky flies at a picnic. But she was wrong.

"OK, I'll send them right up," she said.

She hung up and asked them to sign in on the visitor's log.

"I don't know who you guys know, but you're in. Someone will be down shortly to take you up to the newsroom."

Cal and Kelly both took seats in the waiting area. Nervous, Cal cracked his knuckles. This was it and he knew it. If he was going to get this story in print, he had to sell it right here – and he had yet to discover the full scope of the story, a fact of which he was certain.

CHAPTER 61

GOLD AWOKE AT 10:30 a.m. after hearing his front door slam. He ditched his morning coffee routine. Gold needed no adrenaline rush; panic and fear made coffee seem like a calming agent. After waiting up late into the night to hear word on the capture of the two reporters, Gold had fallen asleep in his chair.

Gold dialed Yukon's cell number, hoping to get something he hadn't received all night – an answer. The call went straight to voice mail. Gold hung up, realizing that his most trusted ally had vanished and had no intention of ever calling him back. He then called Sheriff Jones to get an update.

"Sheriff, got any news for me?"

"Well, we're still searching for—"

"Still searching? You haven't found those two yet? They're just simpleton reporters! You should have brought them in a long time ago. Put a $250,000 reward out on them – that'll get you some help!"

"Now, Mayor, just calm down. We've got some good men out there. They just need a little bit of time. We're tracking everything we can to locate them. Those two will make a mistake soon enough."

"You just remember, Sheriff, that if I go down, you're going down with me."

"No need for idle threats. We've had close calls before. Once we catch them, there won't be any corroborating evidence. You do have their equipment, right?"

"Got it right here. It was the only thing Yukon did right last night."

"Well, just sit tight. I'll call you when we've apprehended them. My men have been out looking all night. They'll find them."

Gold hung up and threw his phone into his chair, running his hands through his hair.

This should've been over a long time ago! How did it come to this?

He sat back down, wondering if he might need to begin getting his flight bag together. The thought of running made him ill. He had grown to love his wife and kids. He never expected the ultimate cover for his past life of crime to become such a burden in his new ventures. But they were. And it made him more patient than he would've been in the past.

Twelve more hours and then I'm out of here.

It was time for Gold to head to the office, act normal, do his job.

* * *

Mercer sat in his patrol car 15 minutes north of Statenville. He was tired and needed a nap. His eyes were almost asleep when another communication from dispatch woke him up again. Based on the nature of the message, Mercer knew Gold was crawling all over the Sheriff – it was more motivation talk to find Cal and Kelly.

Mercer was growing tired of this. He decided to call Cal again.

* * *

"I'm sorry, but we just can't run your story," Dave Youngman told the two reporters sitting across from him.

Cal sighed and slumped. Without the protection of the press, life was going to get complicated – if there was even a life to return to in Statenville. But he decided not to let the news defeat him.

"Is there anything else we can get that would improve the chances of you running this story?" Cal asked.

"Yeah, there has to be something," Kelly added.

"Well, a confession would be nice," said Youngman, smiling. "Seriously, other than that, we need something besides your anonymous sources. I only trust you because Guy told me to trust you – but if you can't even tell me who your anonymous sources are, I'm going to have a hard time defending you if we get questioned about it. Get me something that proves that you're not just two crazy conspiracy theorists. Prove the conspiracy."

"We'll see what we can do," Cal said, standing up to leave. "Thank you for your time, Mr. Youngman."

Cal took two strides toward the door to show himself out. Kelly followed.

"Call me if you get something else, Cal," Youngman said. "I do think you've got the makings of a great story – but you're just not there yet."

Cal turned toward Youngman and nodded. He thought the most dangerous part of this adventure was over. But apparently, there was still work to do, still a criminal to take down – and he and Kelly only had each other.

CHAPTER 62

WHEN CAL'S PHONE RANG, he didn't recognize the number. As he walked out of the lobby doors of *The Tribune* office, he thought about not answering it for a moment, fearing that some government agency might be trying to track him right now. But the curiosity was too much for him.

"Hello?"

"Cal, is that you?"

"Yes – who is this?"

"It's Mercer from the Statenville Sheriff's Department. Don't hang up – just hear me out."

"OK, make it quick, but I've done nothing wrong and I'm not coming in to face some trumped up charges."

"Well, that's kind of why I'm calling. I want to help you."

"I'm listening."

"OK, I know that Mayor Gold was trying to kill you and Kelly last night. Is she with you?"

"Why do you ask?"

"It's important. I need both of you to help me catch Gold."

"Catch Gold? You? What for?"

"Well, Cal, I'm not exactly who I appear to be. I'm actually in deep cover with Buddy Walker, God rest his soul."

"What? Walker's dead?"

"Yeah, the body count is getting unusually high around here –

and you know Gold wanted to add you to that number, right?"

"Yeah, so get to your point. I'm losing patience here."

"OK, listen. I know you're trying to write a story on all of this, but I want to help you win a Pulitzer."

Cal laughed. "OK, that'd be nice, but I'm willing to settle for something unusual for my clips file."

"How about Gold confessing to murder?"

"Murder? Who did he kill?"

"Walker, for starters. But he also killed someone else you know..."

Cal's heart stopped. There was only one person – other than the woman he was standing next to – that would've motivated him to risk his life to catch Gold. Then Mercer uttered his name.

"Guy Thompson."

Cal dropped to the ground. The phone fell out of his hand, too, spinning on the concrete below with the same speed as his racing mind.

How could this happen? This is my fault. He was the only one protecting me.

Only the ambient sounds of Fourth Street were being transmitted back to Mercer.

"What's wrong, Cal?" Kelly asked, kneeling beside him and placing her hand on his back. "What happened?"

Cal looked down and shook his head. "They killed Guy."

Kelly began sobbing. Cal finally released some tears, too. They shared a short embrace and wiped back their tears.

"Kelly, we've got to nail Gold. He can't get away with this."

She nodded. "Whatever we need to do, I'm in."

Cal had almost forgotten about Mercer until he heard a voice coming from his phone, which was now a foot away on the sidewalk.

"Cal? Cal? You there?"

Cal slowly picked up the phone.

"I'm here."

"Listen, Cal. I'm really sorry for your loss. I know Guy was a great man and a good newspaper editor."

"He was an amazing man – and I'm not going to let his death

be for naught. How do we get Gold to confess to murder?"

"OK, great. Well, I was thinking that I could bring you two in so he wouldn't suspect anything. Then, I would call him over and you could have a private moment with him, get him to tell you he did it. Then I would turn around and arrest him and we'd all get what we wanted."

"Why are you doing this, Mercer?"

"Well, I like you, Cal. And I like Kelly. And I really liked Walker, my partner. I wouldn't want his name to be tarnished forever. What he did was wrong, lacing those drugs that ended up killing those boys. But he was just trying to do the right thing. I wouldn't want his relatives to think he was a killer instead of a man who fought for justice."

"Fair enough. Sounds like a good plan. You'll have to come get us. We'll be at the FBI offices in Salt Lake City."

"I'm on my way. I'll call you in two hours when I get there."

Cal hung up and exhaled. He was tired. And angry. And broken. His mentor was murdered all because Cal couldn't stop with this story. Guilt crept over him. Cal started crying again.

"It's all my fault," Cal said, trying to regain his composure.

Kelly teared up again as well. "No, it's not, Cal. You can't blame yourself for what one monster did to Guy. He chose to help us. We lost a good friend today, but let's think of him as a man who sacrificed his life for the truth to be known – and let's figure out a way to survive and tell this story so we can properly honor him."

Cal nodded. He wiped his tears with the back of his hand and got up. He would have to put the full gamut of his emotions on hold. He needed to talk with Mr. Youngman.

CHAPTER 63

"**DO YOU THINK THIS** will work?" Kelly asked Cal.

"I hope so," he said. "It's the best idea that has come to me."

Cal and Kelly went over their own plan as they waited for Mercer to arrive. They trusted him. What other motivation could he have? But Cal was growing up fast. His cub status as a reporter was transitioning to veteran with every twist and turn during his efforts to gather everything he needed to write an accurate story. Cal hoped he was right about Mercer, but he couldn't ignore any inklings that said otherwise. Hopefully, his precautionary measures would be enough, should it come to that.

Cal's heart remained heavy, even as he stole a few glances at Kelly. She was beautiful and he wanted to think about a future with her – but he couldn't. The grief over losing his mentor was too strong, the wound too fresh. Once he did justice for Guy, maybe he could dream of a future with Ms. Mendoza. But for now, there was only one thing he had space in his mind for – catching Gold and telling a story that was so unbelievable Cal scarcely believed it himself. But he knew it was real. People he knew were dead, and he had escaped with his life – so far.

Mercer finally arrived, pulling his squad car to the edge of the designated street curb so Cal and Kelly could get in. They both climbed into the backseat.

***

The two-hour drive back to Statenville was rather uneventful, except for the speed at which it was made. Mercer again offered his condolences to Cal and Kelly over Guy's death. Then Mercer began going over the plan, making sure everyone knew exactly what they were supposed to do.

Mercer explained how he had easily won the trust of Mayor Gold, who became excited when he heard Mercer had captured the pair thanks to a random tip from Salt Lake City. That was far from the truth, but Cal didn't mind. Cal loathed lying and preferred Mercer to do such dirty work. In a short time, Cal knew he was going to have to deceive Gold. But he was confident he could pull it off. This was for Guy.

Ten minutes outside of Statenville, Mercer decided to talk through their plan once more. Cal and Kelly went through it and knew exactly how everything was going to play out. Mercer told them they were both ready. Kelly reached over and squeezed Cal's leg just above his knee.

"You can do this," she said.

"I know I can. I'm going to make Guy proud."

Cal and Kelly both began growing nervous, even though they knew everything they were supposed to do. Cal tried to crack his knuckles, which he found more difficult since he was wearing handcuffs. He took a deep breath in an attempt to remain calm.

Suddenly, Mercer locked all the doors and jerked the steering wheel, making a sharp right turn away from Statenville. The plan had changed.

* * *

Mercer's plan changed hadn't changed that suddenly. It only changed when he realized that Cal and Kelly knew everything – and there weren't going to be any heroes in their story. This was unfortunate for Cal and Kelly. Instead of helping the reporters out, Mercer was driving them to their death. Not that he was going to kill two innocent people – Mercer knew that Gold wanted to oversee the reporters' deaths himself. Just collateral damage.

Then and only then would Mercer make his own move on Gold. Mercer would be the hero, single-handedly busting the mastermind of the great Northwest drug ring – and a wanted mob hit man. Mercer's reputation and the nobility of the FBI would be held in the highest regard. After all, this was all for the greater good.

CHAPTER 64

MAYOR GOLD POSITIONED HIS car in the exact spot he had held less than 24 hours ago. Except this time, Gold knew Cal and Kelly would be in the back of Mercer's squad car. Finally, his nightmare would end once the two reporters' dead bodies hit the bottom of Cold River Canyon. The accident awaiting the two reporters was a rock climbing mishap.

The afternoon sun was harsh in the rock faces. Though standing in scorching August heat was a small sacrifice for Gold. He had long since proved his resolve in protecting Statenville and the drug empire he had concocted.

He smiled as he saw Mercer's patrol car swing into view down the winding dusty road leading to the canyon's edge. No vanishing act was necessary – not for him, anyway. Gold's fondness for his family had begun to blur the bigger picture for him. Not that it was a bad thing, but it was definitely a weakness. Gold knew it, too. However, he never played it safe, choosing to prance upon the ledge of danger. It was an exhilarating place to be, though Gold had yet to feel the effects of falling off. He always pushed those thoughts out of his mind. He could always run and re-invent himself. But not this time. He preferred to stand pat and build something that was lasting – yet it wasn't family he valued *this* deeply.

In a matter of moments, his fortress would become that much more impenetrable.

***

Mercer picked up Cal and Kelly and exchanged a few pleasantries before driving. Cal didn't feel like talking and Mercer seemed content to drive in silence.

After two hours of riding, Cal looked at Kelly and shook his head. All along he had been hoping that he wasn't about to be led into a trap, but here he was. He didn't even bother protesting to Mercer. Cal knew he had been duped. At least he was prepared for it this time.

Mercer broke the awkward silence.

"So, I guess you've figured out we're not going to Gold's office."

"Yeah, I'm not stupid."

"Says who?" Mercer said, nervously cackling at his one liner. "And, oh, you won't be needing this," Mercer added as he picked up Cal's iPhone off the front seat and whipped it out the window and into the canyon below. "Don't worry, the mayor will let you go look for it in a minute."

Mercer chuckled again. Cal couldn't believe just how dark Mercer really was, how cold and calculating he had become in the past minute. He decided not to react, not to give Mercer the pleasure of knowing he was bothered or scared.

Finally, the car skidded to a stop along the remote dusty road. With the exception of Gold, there was no one around this portion of Cold River Canyon, a spot considered the beginning of the Idaho wilderness area.

CHAPTER 65

CAL DIDN'T TAKE MERCER for an opportunistic FBI agent, the kind who would abuse his power for a cut of a hefty payday. But neither did he think Buddy Walker was even an FBI agent. But the biggest shock thus far came when he learned that Mayor Gold was actually one Carmen Deangelo, a top captain from the Scarelli mob family who had disappeared years ago. Before talking with directors at the FBI field office in Salt Lake City, Cal had no idea who the Scarellis were – but they sounded tough. Then one director shared just how ruthless Gold was before he left Boston.

While waiting at the FBI offices for Mercer, Cal had learned from an FBI agent that Mercer and Walker were both being investigated for being a mole. Walker's secret was buried with him, but Mercer might still prove to be the man the FBI was searching for. But mole or no mole, Cal was convinced the primary reason the FBI would be so willing to help a reporter was because they wanted to downplay the fact that one of their agents was directly responsible for the deaths of three high school student-athletes in their prime. They wanted to control the story and spin it their way. Cal wasn't going to play that game, but in the moment, he considered it best to gather all the evidence possible and make judgment calls later on which promises to keep.

In his briefing prior to Mercer's arrival, Cal and Kelly's FBI liaison made it clear that surviving Gold in a situation where he may turn desperate wasn't a guarantee. There were risks involved, serious risks. But Kelly didn't mind. She let it be known just how determined she was to see Gold brought in that Cal never had a chance to even ponder backing out. The FBI was willing to put its full resources into protecting them. It was an opportunity the FBI couldn't pass up, snuffing out a mobster on the FBI's most wanted list and taking down a large drug ring in one shot. They might even catch a mole, too.

For this particular Salt Lake City field office, Cal's scenario represented a gift worthy of being wrapped under the tree at Christmastime by Saint Nick himself. All that remained was for Cal and Kelly to slip down the chimney with ease.

* * *

Cal and Kelly reluctantly got out of the car. Mercer was shoving them around. Cal and Kelly did their best to feign shock and surprise at the double-cross. They played off the part that was genuine, the part they thought would never happen. Plan B was in full force.

Gold got out of his car and walked slowly toward the reporters, whose backs were a safe 15 yards away from the cliff's edge. With outstretched arms and a mischievous grin across his face, Gold appeared to be enjoying the moment. Two reporters who were trying to ruin his life were in handcuffs.

"At last, the two burrs in my saddle are here with me – and I get to crush them myself."

Cal knew he didn't have much time, so he began following the script.

"Burrs in your saddle?" Cal asked. "What are you talking about? I was just trying to figure out what killed your son. I didn't realize I would become such a burr in your saddle for doing my job."

"All reporters are scum. Your job represents about the most debased profession in our society. Reporters are always burrs in my saddle when they go poking their noses where they shouldn't."

"I'm happily guilty then."

"And so am I," Kelly chimed in as her nostrils flared. She was anxious to engage the real scum.

"Oh, a feisty one," Gold said, looking at Kelly. "I always did like you, Kelly. Such a mouth, though. I wonder how well you'll hold your tongue as you fall to the bottom of the canyon."

Gold moved closer toward his intended targets. He reached Cal and grabbed him by his upper arm. Then he looked at Kelly.

"Want to see a man fly?" Gold asked.

Kelly glared at him, wisely choosing to hold her tongue.

Cal decided that remaining silent was to his detriment – and it certainly wasn't in the plan.

"So, you think killing us is going to end the threat of you getting arrested and Cloverdale Industries shut down?"

Gold laughed.

"Absolutely. After all, I've got all your physical evidence. Your word of mouth testimony is weak, but I don't like taking chances."

"You really think that we didn't make any copies?"

"Ha! I know you're bluffing. You've watched too many detective shows, Mr. Cub Reporter. There's no way you had time to get them anywhere else. I destroyed the photos and the photo card myself."

"You've got a lot of confidence, Gold – it's going to be your undoing."

"And your mouth is going to be yours. Well, that and the fact that you're in handcuffs and I'm not."

Gold pulled out a handgun and pointed it toward Cal.

Cal knew he was running out of time and it was time for his final attempt to get a confession from Gold.

"Before you kill me, don't you want to know, Mayor?" Cal said.

"Know what?"

"Know how your son and his two teammates went from being healthy teens one day to dead the next, dead in the most gruesome way?"

Gold kept his gun aimed at Cal's head but played along.

"I hadn't really cared about the reasons why once I realized my son's death meant that Statenville and Cloverdale Industries were about to lose everything I had worked to build. Protecting what was left remained the most important thing. I have other family members who are still alive and need consideration."

"What if I told you that you could avenge his death today along with killing us right here – a three-in-one deal?"

"Go on."

"Do you really need me to spell it out for you?"

"Mercer?"

"Yep. He's the one responsible for your son's death."

Mercer bowed up and began protesting. "You're lying, Cal," he yelled. "Gold, this kid is just trying to save himself. He's full of it!"

"I don't believe you, Cal," Gold said.

Mercer immediately relaxed, but Cal didn't stop.

"Oh, you don't believe me? Well, maybe you should ask Mercer about CPZ. He may have some on him right now."

"What are you talking about?"

"I'm talking about an FBI program to develop markers to mix into batches of drugs. It leads to a strange itching phenomenon that lands a person in the hospital. The strange phenomenon gets reported back to the CDC and the FBI gathers the information to gain knowledge of a drug operation's network. That's what Walker and Mercer were doing in Statenville, helping build a case to take down Cloverdale Industries. And they were gathering enough evidence to put you away forever."

"But Mercer is in my pocket. I've been around long enough to know how to spot a federal agent when I see one – and also how to identify who can be bought. Mercer worked out great – and he has brought you two to me."

"Yeah, but that still doesn't change the fact that he killed your son when he inserted those chemicals into the drugs your son took. He was trying to help you. I guess your son was just collateral damage – an unintended consequence."

"Yes, I'm sure it was unintended. It was most unfortunate, but I know Mercer was trying to help me."

"Yeah, I'm sure your son would've appreciated knowing you thought his life was just collateral damage as he clawed himself to death."

"What are you talking about?"

"You really don't know, do you? How your son died? You're not the least bit curious?"

"Go ahead."

"When added to meth, CPZ begins working on the liver, forcing bile into the blood stream. When it gets into the blood stream, it creates a powerful itching sensation. Except, the itching can't be satiated on the surface. The itching is under your skin. Your son scratched himself to death, enduring some of the worst agony in his final few minutes on this earth. All thanks to Mercer here."

"Mercer, is this true?"

"Like you said, Mayor, I was just trying to help protect Cloverdale and throw off the feds. I never meant for your son to get hurt."

"Besides, how do you know Mercer is really on your side?" Cal added, confident he had said enough to send Gold into a more passionate rage.

As Cal predicted, Gold began redirecting his anger toward Mercer. He pointed his gun at Mercer and began walking toward him. Cal shot Kelly a glance as they both watched his display of aggression in awe.

Mercer slowly walked backward. He was only 10 feet from the edge of the cliff.

"Hey, now. Come on, Gold. You know it was just an unfortunate coincidence. I never meant for your family to get hurt, much less killed."

"You killed my son," Gold said. Anger and hate had given way to a look of vengeance. "He scratched himself to death. You can't die much worse than that – except maybe nursing a blown off knee cap as you plummet to your death."

And with that, Gold fired two shots, one into each of Mercer's knees. Mercer screamed as he staggered toward the ground, a mere three feet from the edge of the cliff. But before Mercer could fall flat, Gold rushed him and gave him a shove with his left foot. Already off balance, Mercer staggered backward again until he reached back to find safe ground and came up empty.

Mercer's scream was piercing for 10 seconds, filling up the canyon with his pain and final last words.

Gold watched Mercer writhe in pain on his way down for a few seconds until he was satisfied that survival was impossible. He then returned his attention to Cal.

"Is that how you did it in Boston – well, except with a gold coin?"

Gold looked stunned for the first time during this encounter. Cal had hoped for such a stunning reaction earlier when he revealed that Mercer was the one who killed Gold's son, but it was mild compared to this.

"Excuse me? What did you say?"

"You heard me. But I'll ask you again: Is that how you did it in Boston? You know, how you murdered people – ruthlessly, inflicting as much pain as possible?"

"Wow, I really underestimated you, Cal. I had no idea you were such a thorough reporter. It's a shame that you're never going to get that career of yours going."

Gold pointed his gun again in Cal's direction.

"I wouldn't recommend that if I were you – because it'll be the last thing you do. Killing me and Kelly, that is."

Gold laughed. "You sure do talk big, Cal. I'll just have you know that you can chalk up your death to that big mouth of yours."

Gold then pointed his gun again at Cal.

"You might want to rethink what you're doing, Gold. I mean, you might be wondering where that red dot on your shirt comes from."

Gold looked down to see a laser site pointed directly at his heart. He'd be dead in less than 30 seconds after a bullet pierced his heart. And he knew it. But he still held the gun on Cal.

"I would just put the gun down in less than two seconds or else you won't have a hand any more," Cal said.

Gold laughed and ignored Cal. Two seconds later, a sniper's A3 G bullet nearly separated Gold's hand from the rest of his body. His handgun fell to the ground.

"It's over, Gold. Give it up."

It *was* over. Cal could tell Gold had conceded by the look on his face. But this wasn't the way Gold wanted to go out, rotting away in prison before getting the death penalty. Endlessly parading into courtrooms wearing shackles and an orange jumpsuit – it wasn't his style.

Gold's hand was gushing blood. He bent over, grabbing his right hand with his left in a worthless attempt to stop the bleeding.

"You ruined everything! You were supposed to be under control."

"Sheriff Jones couldn't do the job?" Cal asked, fishing for a confession.

"Jones isn't an asset, but he could've been a liability had I not included him."

Cal smiled. A corruption trifecta – municipal government, local law enforcement and the FBI. This was perfect.

"I hope you're happy, Cal – and you too, Kelly. You two have ruined my family's life. My kids will grow up without a father. Nice work, scumbags."

Kelly grinned. Then Cal mocked Gold with a sarcastic laugh, this time at Gold's inability to reason.

"Me? Ruined lives? Consider the untold thousands of people you've laid waste to – individuals and families. All these drug users and people you've thrust into a life of crime – yeah, I'm a scumbag for ruining your family's life, a family you only started as a cover."

Gold grimaced, still trying in vain to stop the gushing blood. "It started out that way, but something changed along the way."

"Yeah, it changed all right. You didn't even mourn the loss of your son. He was merely collateral damage."

Gold looked up at Cal and glared. "You don't know anything."

"I know you're going to jail, Gold. It'll be much safer than me dropping a letter with your whereabouts in the mail to the Scarelli family and letting them take you back to Boston – with the FBI's blessing, of course."

"Like I said, you don't know anything."

With that parting shot, Gold turned and leaped out into the canyon, joining Mercer in the cruelest of deaths.

Cal and Kelly both sighed in relief.

"Did you get all this?" Kelly asked, contorting her body to get her hands in a position to pull her iPhone out of her pocket and signal to the FBI sniper situated on top of a ridge. "Now, get down here and take these handcuffs off us."

After meeting with Cal and Kelly earlier in the day, the FBI flew a sniper along with a full tactical team to a spot overlooking Gold's favorite dumping ground at Cold River Canyon. While the FBI suspected that Mercer might be the mole, they decided to discreetly record all the events with Kelly's iPhone, a device nobody knew she still possessed. The open line also allowed the tactical team to know how to react to the events happening in front of them. Mercer's motives remained a mystery to the bureau, but it didn't matter now.

Had both Gold and Mercer survived, FBI officials knew any admission of guilt by Gold in this situation would likely wilt when held up to the law. But a revealing story written by a news organization could have forced Gold to make a desperate move – and that was when they knew the bureau could catch him. All that guess work, speculation and theory vanished in about ten seconds when Gold killed Mercer – and then it all became moot when Gold leaped himself. No FBI officials were complaining.

For the second time in less than 24 hours, Cal and Kelly avoided being flung to the bottom of Cold River Canyon.

CHAPTER 66

RIDING BACK TO SALT Lake City in a government-issued SUV, Cal finally felt safe. Kelly did, too. Their adventure together over the past three days seemed surreal, something neither would have expected living in Statenville. But this wasn't just adventure for adventure's sake – this was about uncovering the truth and finding justice. It was hard work but rewarding work.

However, one question still remained: Could Cal and Kelly put together a story package with photos and videos that would find its way into print. A story of such depth and magnitude deserved a stage much larger than *The Register*. Then again, neither Cal nor Kelly knew if they had a job there any more. Not that they could seriously consider working in a town where their investigation ruined almost everyone's livelihood in a direct or indirect way.

Cal felt the pressure to deliver.

Following a debriefing with FBI officials at the Salt Lake City field office, Cal pleaded with them to wait until morning to announce the death of Carmen Deangelo and the bust of Cloverdale Industries. Cal explained that his story would demonize only Mercer, not Walker. After a few minutes of haggling over the details, the FBI relented, considering that Cal had risked his life. It was the least they could do to thank him.

Nevertheless, Cal was ecstatic, excited about the challenge that awaited him in the coming hours. He and Kelly caught a cab to the *The Tribune* office and briefed Youngman on what had transpired. It was 6:30 p.m.

"OK, you've got two hours to write an exclusive for us that's well sourced," Youngman said.

"You got it – except for the exclusive part. Seattle is getting this story, too," Cal said.

"Anyone else?" Youngman asked.

"Not as of right now."

"Let's keep it that way. Get my assistant to find you a workstation. And have Kelly meet with the photo chief," Youngman shouted as he was leaving the office.

Cal's story that appeared in two newspapers the next day read as follows:

By Calvin J. Murphy
For The Tribune

STATENVILLE, Idaho – FBI officials confirmed the death of long-standing Boston mobster Carmen Deangelo on Wednesday when Deangelo plummeted to his death in Cold River Canyon after murdering an FBI agent.

Deangelo, who was living under the assumed name of Nathan Gold, had almost vanished before moving to Statenville in 1996. FBI officials claim that Gold established himself as a respectable member of the community before running for mayor eight years ago.

But Deangelo wasn't leaving behind his life of crime – he was building a new one.

In 2001, two years prior to Deangelo being elected as the mayor of Statenville, he founded Cloverdale Industries, a fast-growing, multi-level marketing company that sold mostly vitamins and health products. When Gold assumed the mayor's office in 2003, the FBI asserts that everything was in place for him to build an extensive distribution network for crystal meth in the Northwest.

"The death of Carmen Deangelo represents a major victory in the FBI's war on drugs," FBI Salt Lake City field office director Skip Donnelly was quoted as saying in a press release Wednesday. "Any time we can scratch a name off the FBI's most wanted list, it's a win for the American people. This particular removal of Carmen Deangelo's name is a bigger victory than anyone could've ever imagined."

FBI officials claim that Deangelo was the architect behind a vast drug operation that spread as far north as Vancouver, Canada, and east as far as Denver.

Deangelo stayed off the FBI's radar for nearly 15 years. Then, in 2005, the FBI was alerted that Deangelo might be returning to his criminal ways after a known drug dealer's body was found in Portland with Deangelo's signature mark—a gold coin from the 1800s stuffed in the victim's mouth. It was the same signature Deangelo used for most of his alleged murders in Boston.

The FBI deployed two agents to Statenville to serve in deep cover and build a case against Deangelo and his Cloverdale Industries. The plan went awry beginning Sunday evening when the first of three local high school football stars were found dead in gruesome crime scenes.

The deaths rocked the quiet southeastern Idaho town. Residents were told that the student-athletes all overdosed on meth, but local law enforcement officials pressured the coroner's office to release falsify reports.

But on Tuesday, an independent examination of evidence by FBI officials found the cause of death to be markers the meth was laced with, not the meth itself. The markers were supposed to induce what appeared like the sudden onset of a rare disease, which would alert the Center for Disease Control and subsequently the FBI. But the marker was never intended to be fatal, according to the FBI. The chemical was a marker that deep cover FBI agents were supposed to insert into random batches of drugs to track how far the operation's network extended.

However, a rogue FBI agent undermined those efforts by engineering the additive to have a deadly effect – forcing liver bile into the bloodstream quickly, which led to uncontrollable itching beneath the skin. Already high from using meth, all three victims scratched themselves to death. One of the victims happened to be Riley Gold, Deangelo's son.

Nevertheless, Gold and local law enforcement officials didn't want to attract unwarranted attention to Statenville and chose to dismiss the deaths as coincidence.

But the case hit a fever pitch on Wednesday when the FBI had an opportunity to illicit a confession out of Deangelo in a covert operation. However, Deangelo chose to take his own life, plummeting into the Cold River Canyon at the southern part of the Idaho wilderness area instead of facing charges. Just moments before, Deangelo had killed FBI agent Elliott Mercer, wounding him with two gunshots before shoving him off a cliff and into the canyon.

Deangelo was suspected in the murders of more than a dozen people while living in Boston as a captain for the Scarelli family.

FBI officials have also seized control of Cloverdale Industries and have shut down operations until the bureau completes its investigation of the alleged drug making plant.

***

Cal's journalistic efforts delighted Youngman, who edited in the details of how the case related to Salt Lake City – the drugs were flowing into the city from Cloverdale Industries. The Seattle newspaper did likewise.

It made for a compelling lead story on the front page in both cities, strengthened also by Kelly's compelling photojournalism that captured the images of the people and places involved.

"This is outstanding work from both of you," Youngman told the two former *Register* employees. "I'd love to offer both of you a job, if you're interested."

They both promised Youngman they would consider it, but at the moment, they were crashing hard from the adrenaline rush of the last three days.

The FBI provided a security detail for both Cal and Kelly, putting them up in separate safe houses that night. It was only a safety precaution FBI agents told them, adding that there was likely nothing to worry about. But the security presence helped Cal and Kelly both sleep well that night. They needed it – an awkward reunion with Statenville awaited them on Thursday morning.

CHAPTER 67

WHEN CAL AND KELLY walked through the doors of *The Register's* office late Thursday morning, the handful of employees remaining stood and clapped. News traveled fast, though the magnitude of such news in Statenville warranted a special edition. But it was an edition that would never get printed.

Guy was gone and FBI agents combed the publisher's office for anything that could link him to the illegal activity going on with Gold and Cloverdale Industries. Joseph Mendoza was destined to lose control of the paper due to his ties to Gold. Sammy Mendoza would likely find some jail time, too – not the ideal candidate to take over the family business. If Kelly chose to stay in Statenville, it looked increasingly likely that the keys to the Mendoza treasure trove – *The Register* – would be handed to her at a young age.

Daniel Richardson, one of *The Register's* board members, greeted Cal and Kelly. He informed the pair of the plans to restructure the newsroom, offering Kelly the role of publisher and Cal the title of executive editor. It was another decision that needed time.

Cal thought it sounded like a romantic idea – marrying Kelly, settling down in a small town, and making *The Register* a trusted source of information again. But as much as Cal liked the thought of it all, the idea that he would have to stay in Statenville – cow town, Idaho, as he liked to call it – for the rest of his life wasn't so appealing. Maybe it wouldn't have to be that way. Maybe he could have his dream girl *and* his dream job. They could investigate more corrupt politicians and governments together and win a few Pulitzers …

But that wasn't really Cal's dream, the kind he had an opportunity to seize right now. His deepest professional desire was to cover professional sports for a large metro daily newspaper, not write grip-and-grin cutlines for a podunk weekly. He wanted to talk about the Super Bowl at dinner parties *after* he returned from covering the event. He wanted to share his opinion in columns and online for websites – and have fans talk about *his* thoughts on whatever particular subject he decided to broach. He had long given up the idea that he would play in the NFL after he tapped out at an average 5-foot-9 and 160 pounds wearing winter clothes. Cal's dream of covering an NFL team still remained a attainable. And it was too early to determine if it was worth sacrificing that dream for Kelly.

Cal sat down at his desk and began going through his papers and notebooks. He knew that he wasn't long for this job or this town. *The Tribune* job was a nice offer, but it wasn't a sportswriter job; though it was far better in pay and exposure than anything *The Register* had to offer – even at the executive level.

His iPhone buzzed, slowly walking across his desk. It was Josh.

"Hey, Josh. How are you?"

"I'm all right, but probably not as good as you, Mr. Scoop."

"So, *The Times* ran my story there in Seattle?"

"Oh, did we. It dominated the front page of today's paper. Why didn't you tell me you were working on this?"

"Probably because nothing started happening until the moment I hung up with you on Monday."

"Impressive. You'll have to tell me all about it this weekend."

"You're still coming?"

"You better believe it. I wouldn't miss thrilling eight-man football action on Friday night for all the taters in Idaho."

"Great. I'll see you tomorrow at the airport."

Cal couldn't believe it. A conversation – albeit a short one – that did not include one single insult from Josh. It was a first.

"Who was that?" Kelly asked.

"Oh, that was my friend Josh. He's coming into town this weekend. You'll have to meet him."

"Aww, that's too bad. I've got other plans. I'm going on a fly fishing trip with my dad this weekend. Maybe he can help me figure out what to do with my life and this opportunity here."

"Sounds like fun. Have a good time. Let me know what you decide."

Kelly laughed. "What? You want to know if I'm going to be the publisher or not so you can decide if you want to work for me?"

"No, it's not that. I'm just wondering what I'm going to do and I'd like to hear your thoughts."

"Don't worry – I'll share them with you as soon as I know something. We do make a great team though."

"I can't argue with that."

Cal wondered if he was at a crossroads in his life or a simple fork. Maybe those paths would converge again one day – or maybe they would branch out in opposite directions never to intersect again. Everything was uncertain for Cal. But it was a good uncertainty, the kind most people wished they had again when life was still unscripted.

Cal knew tough decisions were ahead.

CHAPTER 68

AT 7 A.M. ON FRIDAY morning, Cal got up and checked his email before driving to the Boise airport to pick up Josh. Cal still loathed getting up with the sun, but Josh had selected a morning flight, leaving him no choice but to join the ranks of the early risers.

Cal's in-box overflowed with requests for interviews from media outlets across the country. They all wanted to know how he learned of Carmen Deangelo's identity, and what kind of reaction the people of Statenville had regarding their mayor's sordid past and subsequent death. One boring request for his time after another – except for one.

The producer from the "Mitch in the Morning" show on 950-AM KJR in Seattle wanted to see if Cal would be interested in joining Mitch for 10 minutes at some point that morning to discuss the death of quarterback Cody Murray. It was the one angle Cal had wanted to tell but didn't have the right opportunity. Finally, a venue to properly eulogize an outstanding quarterback, one who had a surprising future for a player on an eight-man team. He replied right away, even though the show was nearly an hour old.

Cal's iPhone rang 30 seconds later with the show producer giving him specific instructions on what to do. The producer wanted him on in 15 minutes since one of the other guests – a well-known Major League star – had cancelled on Mitch due to an unforgiving night on the town the previous evening. Cal was happy to fill the spot.

Cody had received offers from Eastern Washington and Boise State, but there were rumors that Oregon State and Washington were also interested in the dual-threat quarterback. It was Mitch's way of stealing the city's hottest story that morning and giving it a sports angle to attract more listeners. Besides, he was the only one with the reporter who had a front-row seat to all the mayhem.

Cal was insightful and flawless during his interview with Mitch. The 10-minute scheduled interview turned into 20 minutes of compelling radio with a break in between. Cal was so interesting that Mitch even delayed an interview with Seattle Seahawks head coach Pete Carroll for five minutes – and Mitch even allowed Cal to encourage listeners to follow him on Twitter. Mitch's producer had to come up with a plausible excuse for Carroll to wait, instead of telling him that the guy on the air right now is really good. When Cal's interview was over, his iPhone buzzed again.

"Hey, Cal. Just wanted to let you know that Mitch loved you – and he wanted to know if you'd be interested in talking about recruits from Idaho throughout the fall, on occasion."

"Sure, I'd love to. You know how to find me."

Cal hung up and smiled. He didn't know how he could get a foot in the competitive Seattle sports market, but in one phone call, he was in with both feet – without really trying. He checked his email account again before heading out. His seven loyal Twitter followers were now part of a legion of 80 that had suddenly appeared since his interview. Cal couldn't wait to tell Josh.

Before getting up from his desk, Cal noticed one more email that piqued his interest. He began reading:

Cal,

I just wanted to thank you for finding out the truth about Cody, Devin and Riley's deaths. They deserved as much, even though it was their own senseless actions that cost them their lives in a way. The few people who love Statenville for what it was, not for what it has become, will grieve their deaths – and celebrate the return of the real Statenville, the one that was built on the backs of hard-working men and women as opposed to some drug scam.

I'm sure you'll have job offers galore after doing such a thorough job of covering this story that supposedly wasn't. But I just thought you should know from a Statenville old timer that you did us proud.

Best of luck wherever you go!

Warmest Regards,

Coach Mike Miller

Cal wasn't sure which was harder to secure – a Pulitzer or a compliment from anyone, much less someone you tried to objectively cover on a regular basis. Either way, Coach Miller's email might as well have been a Pulitzer to Cal. He printed it out. It was something else he couldn't wait to show Josh.

***

At the Boise airport, Cal awaited Josh's arrival inside. He hated driving around waiting on people to deplane or waiting in the cell phone lot. Besides, Cal thought if he was picking up anyone from the airport, it had to be a real friend or a family member. He wasn't a chauffeur. Even chauffeurs parked their limos and went inside to personally greet their clients – the idea of a cell phone lot was absurd. Cal always felt greeting someone inside was the personable thing to do.

When Josh came through the glass doors, Cal greeted him with a handshake and then a hug – one that emphasized they were close friends but nothing more than that. The three rhythmic pats on the back that came in unison verified as much – "We're (pat) just (pat) friends (pat)".

"It's good to see you, Josh."

"Good to see you too, Cal." Josh immediately turned the conversation toward a more serious tone. "How are you doing?"

"What do you mean?"

"I mean, with all the things you went through over the past week, how are you doing? Are you crazy now? Was it hard going through that? Did you think you were going to die?"

Josh paused before lightening the serious mood.

"Is your rookie Ken Griffey Jr. card bequeathed to me in your will?"

Cal chuckled. "All cards are going to you, Josh. But seriously,

260 | R.J. PATTERSON

I'm doing all right. I try not to think about the fact that Kelly and I were almost murdered and dumped into the bottom of a canyon – and maybe not in that order. When I do think about it, it's like an out-of-body experience. I see myself doing things I wouldn't naturally think to do."

"It's just amazing what you did. And your story had our whole newsroom buzzing."

"Really?"

"Yes, really. It also had my editors buzzing, especially when I told them I was flying out to meet you today and that you were one of my friends from college. They wanted me to give you something."

Josh extended an envelope with *The Times* logo and address on it. Cal grabbed it and began opening it.

"What is it?"

"It's an offer for you to come work as an enterprise reporter on our sports staff."

"Are you serious?" Cal jumped up and down a few times before giving Josh a hug without regard for how anyone viewed their relationship. Josh almost lost his balance in all the elation.

"Yeah, I'm serious. After your story came through, I mentioned that we were friends and reminded the sports staff that I beat you out for the internship – to which I received many wise cracks, most of which were completely demeaning toward me. Our sports editor then dug up your resume and asked me if I thought you'd want to work in sports."

"What did you tell him?"

"I told him yes, of course. An hour later, they gave me this envelope and told me to give it to you when I saw you today."

"Wow! All I can say is thanks! We're going to be together again."

"Well, not so fast. I'm not sure if I'm going to end up staying there after my internship is up next month. It's all up in the air."

"Oh, that's too bad."

"For me – but not for you. You really deserve it, Cal. I mean, anybody that served a sentence at a small town weekly has definitely paid their dues."

"Well, it's not as bad as you might think. I actually met some really nice people in Statenville and learned a lot, thanks to Guy Thompson, God rest his soul."

"That's great. I'm glad it worked out for you."

Josh paused before wading into the touchy subject of women.

"So, what about this Kelly girl? Is there anything to you and her?"

"That is a good question. I really like her, but I'm not sure we've got the same vision for life."

"That's too bad because I've got an offer for her as well to come work for *The Times*."

Cal looked slack-jawed at Josh.

"They offered her a job, too?"

"Yep, sure did. The photo chief was blown away by the amount of quality pictures she took as you guys were fleeing for your lives. Really good photojournalism, from what he said. You think she'll take it?"

"I don't know. Your guess is as good as mine."

"So, you gonna take the job?"

"Probably. I've got a lot to work through after the past few days. I want to weigh all my options, but you know Seattle is where I've wanted to be for as long as I can remember."

"I'll take that as a yes."

Cal smiled and said nothing. He turned onto the interstate and pressed the gas pedal down. He was doing things his way – no compromise, hard work and a stroke of good luck. It hadn't felt that way four days ago. Yet, like a story can turn on the fortune of one good lead, so can one's life. Cal couldn't believe his was turning out to be one such story.

ACKNOWLEDGEMENTS

We write in community and there have been plenty of people who have contributed to this project in one form or another.

Many thanks must first go to my dad, who taught me how to tell a good story, leaving me on the edge of my bed wanting the next snippet of his creative bedtime stories, and my mom, who instilled in me the importance of good grammar to accentuate good written stories.

I also want to acknowledge Joy Pilkington, the woman who taught me how to write and that writing is more than a natural talent – it's an acquired skill.

I appreciate the editorial assistance of Jennifer Wolf and her keen eye in making this book better than it was.

And last but not least, I appreciate my wife for giving me the time to help make this book a reality and for indulging me in hours of conversation about this story and finding ways to make it better.

ABOUT THE AUTHOR

R.J. PATTERSON is an award-winning journalist living in southeastern Idaho with his wife and three children. He likes enjoying the great outdoors of the Northwest and following sports. He also loves connecting with readers and would love to hear from you. To stay updated about future projects, connect with him over Facebook or by visiting his website at www.RJPbooks.com.

Made in the USA
Middletown, DE
12 March 2018